T — 186
250 —

PROVIDENCE

PASS

PROVIDENCE

PASS

Douglas Rawling

iUniverse, Inc.
Bloomington

Providence Pass

This is a work of fiction. All of the characters, names, incidents, organizations, and dialogue in this novel are either the products of the author's imagination or are used fictitiously.

iUniverse books may be ordered through booksellers or by contacting:

iUniverse
1663 Liberty Drive
Bloomington, IN 47403
www.iuniverse.com
1-800-Authors (1-800-288-4677)

ISBN: 978-1-4759-8556-6 (sc)
ISBN: 978-1-4759-8557-3 (e)

Library of Congress Control Number: 2013906684

Printed in the United States of America

iUniverse rev. date: 5/9/2013

CHAPTER ONE

A very Carson stood leaning on the doorjamb of the barbershop watching the busy Dodge City street with complete indifference. The skin on his face tingled from the aftershave, and even in the heat of the afternoon, he was aware of a cool breeze that touched his cheek. It had been a long time between shaves, he reflected—all the way up from Texas. With the long drive over, he now had no idea what to do or where to go. What he knew for certain, though, was that he wasn't going back. That thought had been slowly taking hold over the past few weeks and was now firmly rooted. It was the only thing he knew for sure.

He willed himself into motion and, straightening his tall frame, paused to let a woman and small child pass before stepping from the shade to the sunlit street. The constant hum of life and activity that surrounded him contrasted sharply with his dead spirits, and he felt the need to be away. Picking his way through the traffic, he angled across the street to the Palace Saloon. Though unassuming on the outside, the tavern catered to a higher clientele, and he was pretty sure he'd find Paulson there. Stepping into a cool and quiet room, he spotted his man at a back table, sharing a drink with a couple of well-dressed strangers he assumed were cattle buyers.

Paulson was on the downhill side of middle age, and his beard showed a hint of gray. He carried some extra weight in his belly that even months on the trail couldn't touch, and though one might take him to be soft, Avery knew Paulson was hard as nails.

Avery paused in the doorway; removed his hat; and, out of habit, ran his fingers through his thick, dark hair, though it was now cut too short to make a difference. He was aware that his range clothes were out of place but then decided he didn't care. Paulson had seen him enter and nodded a greeting as the other two gentlemen turned to watch his approach. Ignoring them, Avery slumped into a vacant chair.

"Howdy, Avery. Got cleaned up some I see," Paulson said, concern showing in his eyes.

Avery saw the look and straightened up, ashamed of his weakness. He was a broad-shouldered man with a strong, chiseled face, and most of his life, he had willingly assumed the role of a leader. Usually men looked to him for strength, and until now, he'd seemed to have an unlimited reserve.

"Avery, this here's Graham Thompson," Paulson went on, gesturing with a nod to the man on his left. "This other gent's Karl Wilson. They represent the outfit that's buyin' our cattle. Gentlemen, this is my good friend and neighbor, Avery Carson. The Bar C cattle belong to him."

Avery nodded politely and shook the hands that were offered and then turned to regard Willy Paulson. He waited a moment and then spoke. "Willy, I want you to buy my place."

A look of protest crossed Paulson's brow before he shook his head and said, "Come on, Avery. I can't do that."

"I don't see why not. It's small, but it's a good place. Lord knows you can afford it." Avery leaned forward and placed his forearms on the table and then continued intently, "It's well watered, and the creek will help you make better use of your grass on them north slopes."

"It ain't that, Avery," Paulson said, the other men at the table forgotten. "I know it's a good place. It's just that, well that's your home. Where will you go? You can't run forever."

Avery shot a glance across the table that told Paulson that, even for a good friend, he'd gone too far. "If you won't buy it, then just use it," Avery said speaking crisply. "You can pay me what you think the rent's worth if and when I come back. If you do decide to buy it, we'll settle up later."

For a time no one spoke. Then Paulson said, "When's later?"

"I don't know."

"What are you going to do?"

"I don't know that either." Again there was silence.

Avery pushed back his chair and stood to leave. "You'll take Gibson on?"

Paulson nodded.

"Thanks for everythin', Willy," Avery said in a quiet voice that betrayed deep emotion.

Again Paulson nodded, his eyes troubled.

"Just deposit my share from the sale into my account if you don't mind."

"You got travelin' money?"

"Enough."

With a heavy sigh, Paulson rose to his feet, and the two men shook hands firmly. Avery made to leave and then, pausing in midstride, turned back to face Paulson.

"One other thing, Willy," he said. He swallowed and looked down at the floor as he continued, "Could you put some flowers on her grave from time to time?"

"Sure, Avery. Sure."

Without another word, Avery straightened his shoulders and strode purposefully across the room and out the door.

CHAPTER TWO

It was five days since Avery Carson had last seen another human being, and that was how he wanted it. After leaving Dodge, he'd ridden north to Julesburg, where he'd picked up a packhorse and supplies before following the North Platte to the small settlement of Dickenson Crossing. There he'd spent the night, and the following morning, he'd left the river and struck out in a northwesterly direction. The mountains to the west that had at one time been no more than a faint hint of blue on the horizon now stood stark and clear, towering over the landscape. The tallest of the peaks showed a dusting of new snow, and the leaves on the aspens were beginning to turn.

Not wishing to be seen, Avery was taking care to keep off the skyline. He waited until he reached the steeper timbered slopes to cross over the ridge he was following. He knew he was in Indian country, and though he thought he was too far north to worry about the Kiowa, this would be someone's hunting grounds. He paused to let his horses have a blow and then began his descent to where a silvery creek ran its twisting course down the draw below him. It was early to make camp, but he wanted to have his fire out well before dark so it would not betray his presence.

Later, as the deepening mountain shadows reached eastward toward the plains, he sat with his back against a poplar tree, waiting for the first stars to appear. As had become his custom, the last thing he'd done before dousing his fire was to make a pot of coffee. Because there was no way around it, evening was his time for thought and reflection. For the most part, the challenges of the journey were enough to keep his mind occupied during daylight hours.

He tested his coffee, found it too hot, and set it aside before taking a bite of pan bread. The chill of the evening reminded him that winter was coming, and he'd soon need to make some decisions. It would get a lot colder this far north than what he was used to back home in Texas.

Back home in Texas. He shook his head at the emptiness he felt. He'd always been a man so sure of himself. During his time with the Rangers, he'd seen and done things he'd just as soon not think about, but he'd always believed his actions had been just. "A man reaps what he sows," he'd often said with absolute confidence. If a man's crimes brought him to a violent end, he had no one to blame but himself. Now, he wasn't so sure. Maybe he just couldn't face the fact that he was to blame for what had happened. He'd been so sure the young team would give Audrey no trouble. His last words to her would always haunt him.

"Audrey, you'll be fine. Trust me."

Avery sat morose and brooding, staring at the dead coals of his fire as darkness took the day. He reached for his coffee, and as he did, a dim yellow glow far to the northeast caught his attention. *There must be a settlement down there*, he reasoned. Although he had no desire for human contact, he decided he'd ride that way the following morning. He would take the opportunity to stock up on supplies, and maybe he'd get some idea as to where to spend the winter. He downed the last of his coffee, contemplated pouring himself another cup, but decided he'd heat the rest up in the morning. He checked the horses and then crawled into his bedroll as the moon broke over the eastern horizon.

Morning found him switchbacking his way down a steep grade through a scattering of pines. Here the early sun found the ragged ridges well before it could shed its warmth on the hills below. With a touch of frost, the bunch grass fairly sparkled under his horse's hooves as he broke from the trees. Overhead, the sky was clean and blue.

After skirting a draw to avoid losing unnecessary altitude, Avery scrambled up a brush-covered slope, pulled his horse to a stop, and paused to take in the panoramic view. Here the mountains fell away to the west a good fifteen miles before angling sharply back east. Across a wide valley about ten miles to the north, the range broke off to a steep, grass-covered ridge that shouldered its way well out onto the prairie. Far to the east and at the foot of this ridge, he could make out the faint ribbon of a stage road that meandered through rolling hills speckled with cattle. The town, which he could see clearly now, was built on the bend of a river near the open end of the valley. Looking back west, Avery saw that the river flowed from a distinct notch in the mountains, and beyond that, it appeared the country opened up again, forming another basin higher up.

Avery was surprised at how the scene sparked his interest. The valley before him looked to be a cattleman's paradise, but why he should care, he didn't know. He did know, however, that he wanted to ride through that notch to the west to see what was on the other side. It was the first time in a long time he'd felt motivated by where he wanted to go instead of what he wanted to leave behind. He shrugged his shoulders and tried to forget about it. Nudging his horse into motion, he began picking his way down the slope to the grasslands below.

It was just before noon when Avery splashed across the ford downstream from town. The main street ran east to west, and the sun felt good on his shoulders as he pulled up to the livery barn on the outskirts. The hostler, a skinny, balding man in his late fifties wearing bib overalls, stepped through the double doors as Avery dismounted, smiled a greeting, and said, "Howdy. Want me to off saddle and take care of your pack?"

Avery nodded, and in an expressionless voice that betrayed he was in no mood for small talk, replied, "Sure, thanks."

Conforming to the mood, the hostler replied indifferently, "I'll throw your things in an empty stall. You can stop by and get what you need later."

Hearing the change in tone, Avery glanced at the other man and, making a belated attempt at friendliness, forced a smile and said, "Thanks. Anywhere a man can grab a bite?"

The smile was unseen as the hostler led the horses down the alleyway. Without turning, he responded, "Three doors down, across the street. Bow City Hotel. Only eatin' place in town."

Avery glanced in that direction, spotted the hotel, and angled directly for it across an empty street. A couple of ponies were standing hipshot out front, and two doors down, four more stood in front of a building with a crudely painted sign that simply read "Saloon."

Before entering the hotel, Avery took a moment to study the town. All of the buildings were log, and this was no surprise, as a short distance to the north the grassland rose to meet pine-covered slopes. Directly across the street stood a large building with a boldly painted sign on its false front that read "Bow City Mercantile," and just west of it squatted a low-roofed harness and saddle shop. Next to that was the sheriff's office. Other buildings were scattered in each direction, and by the look of the logs, none of them had been there much more than five years. The town, which he correctly guessed was Bow City, was just wide enough to accommodate two streets running parallel each side of the main street. From what Avery could see, these were sided mostly with houses, although a steeple topped with a cross showed above the buildings furthest west.

Stepping through the door and seeing the registration

desk directly in front of him, Avery decided he may as well take a room before he ate. Beside a bell on the desk was a handwritten sign that read, "Ring for Service." He rang the bell and turned to study two photographs on the wall beside the desk. Photographs were a rare thing, and these were both pictures of mounted cowboys. On the bottom of one picture someone had written, "Slash 7 roundup crew." He recalled that the two ponies out front had been wearing the Slash 7 brand.

Hearing quick steps behind him, Avery turned to see a slender young woman coming through the restaurant door. She wore a plain gray dress with long sleeves and a high collar that was buttoned up tight around her neck. Though drab and unflattering, the dress could not hide the fact that her figure would be the envy of any woman. She had pale blonde hair tied back in a low ponytail, and her pretty face was as striking as her figure. Her blue eyes held a guarded reserve that seemed to melt away when she saw him.

"Ah, a stranger," she said in a friendly voice that seemed to hold a trace of relief. "You must have ridden in, as the stage isn't due for another two days."

Avery realized suddenly that this woman was not just pretty, but that she was truly beautiful. He felt immediately angry that he'd noticed, and he looked quickly away.

Seeing his reaction, the guarded look came back to the woman's face, and she said in a toneless voice, "Room four. Up the stairs and to your right. Sign here, and there's your key. You can pay when you check out." She turned and retreated to the restaurant.

Avery watched her go, sighed heavily, and bent to sign the register.

The restaurant was in a small room with windows that overlooked the street. Three tables lined the side wall, while one longer table occupied the center of the room. Avery hesitated briefly in the doorway, and the pleasant smells from the kitchen put a keen edge on his hunger. The girl in the gray dress was taking an order from a bearded man with thick red hair as Avery crossed the floor to take a seat at the table farthest from the door. As was his habit, he sat with his back to the wall so he could survey the room. Two men sat across from each other at the next table. The man with his back to Avery was dressed in range clothes, and the other fellow looked to be in his mid-fifties. He too was wearing riding gear, but his were cleaner and less worn.

When the waitress turned for the kitchen, Avery couldn't help but notice how the red-haired man stared as she walked away. Soon she was heading for his table, her manner stiff and formal. He wanted to say something to ease the tension, but as was often the case, words failed him, so he said nothing.

She was the one to speak. "That's okay, I don't like you either. There's meat pie, beef with beans, or steak and biscuits."

"I'll try the meat pie."

"Coffee?"

"Yes. Thanks."

She left, and once again, Avery noticed the red-haired

man watching her. Their eyes met, and the other man looked quickly down at his food.

The girl returned shortly with his coffee and a generous piece of steaming pie. She unceremoniously set it in front of him and said, "Let me know if you want seconds."

Avery nodded, and she left.

The food was delicious, but he had to take it slow as it was very hot. When the two riders got up to leave, they glanced his way, but he pretended not to notice. Eventually the redhead left too, and Avery watched him through the window as he crossed the street and disappeared inside the mercantile. The waitress came and filled his coffee, but no words were exchanged, and when his meal was finished, he left the money on the table and headed outside to look for a barber.

About an hour later, he was back on the street, lost for what to do. He'd had a lot of time to think lately, and he realized that he'd developed several habits over time—a way of living that seemed right to him. He'd made a mental note that he was going to do things differently. After all, where had his unwritten code gotten him? For one thing, he seldom drank in the afternoon. That, he'd always reasoned, was a waste of daylight, and with a change in mind, he headed for the saloon. Stepping up onto the boardwalk, he noticed three of the horses out front were branded Slash 7.

The saloon had a low ceiling supported by heavy log beams. It was poorly lit, and a scrawny man in a bowler hat sat under a window near the door playing solitaire with a greasy, dog-eared deck. He looked up as Avery entered, nodded a greeting, and then went back to his game. Three other men sitting at a back table were halfway through a bottle of whiskey with an empty on the floor. They were in quiet conversation over a poker game and threw curious glances Avery's way. He ignored them and walked over to the bar. No barkeep was in sight, but Avery was in no hurry.

"Henry! You got a customer!" one of the cowboys at the table yelled.

Avery turned to regard the speaker, a stocky, round-faced man who smiled, touched his hat brim, and then went back to his cards.

A tall, haggard-looking fellow with big ears and a bobbing Adam's apple stepped through a door behind the bar, wiping his hands on a dirty towel. "What'll it be?" he asked.

"Whiskey."

"Bottle or glass?"

"Glass."

Noting Avery's accent, the bartender said, "Long way from Texas," and poured the whiskey.

Avery nodded. "Long way," he agreed.

"Yell when you need more."

Avery nodded again and then turned his back as the bartender retreated through the door.

"This game could use some fresh money. Want to sit in?" The speaker was the same man who'd called in the barkeep.

Another one of Avery's rules was that he seldom gambled. Money was hard earned and hard to hold on to, and to his thinking, it made no sense to trust it to the whim of the dice or a deck of cards. He hesitated and then grabbed a chair from an empty table. After a few moments of scuffing chairs and moving glasses the cowboys made room for Avery at their table.

"Well, Texas, I'm Fred Staples," the stocky man said. "This here's Crazy Nick; his mama named him somethin' else, but none of us remembers what it is. This other gent's Adam Carns. We all ride for the Slash 7."

Avery nodded and shook hands but didn't offer his name, and if anyone noticed, it was Adam Carns.

"Trailed a herd up from Texas then drifted I'm guessin'," Staples said as he began shuffling the deck.

Avery nodded. "Any other outfits in these parts?" he asked.

"There's the Double Diamond, the Box X, and a few one-horse outfits." This time it was Carns who spoke. "The Slash 7's the biggest though. Are you lookin' for work?"

"I don't know," Avery said honestly. "I guess I'll need to winter somewhere."

"Macy and Rigger just rode out. Too bad you missed them," Staples said.

Avery guessed correctly that of the three, Staples had done the most damage to the empty bottle.

"Macy owns the Slash 7 and Rigger's the foreman," Nick explained. Nick was a tall, narrow-shouldered man with a thick mop of unkempt, black hair that hung ragged over his forehead and shirt collar.

Adam Carns was short, compact, and wiry with careful but friendly eyes.

The talk soon petered out, as the men got down to playing poker. Avery hit a lucky streak right from the start, and at first it was greeted with good-natured banter, but as the cards kept coming his way, the mood began to change.

Avery took another pot, and Staples's whiskey-flushed face twisted in disgust as he knocked back another glass. "So that's how you play friendly poker in Texas, huh," he said as he put down his glass with a little too much force. The more he'd drunk, the bolder he'd played and the worse it had gone for him.

Avery had taken close to fifty dollars of the other men's money, and on cowboy wages, that was a lot. On the next hand, he forced the issue with a pair of sevens, thinking he would lose and could leave the game on better terms. To his dismay, he took the pot again, and he decided enough was enough.

"Well, thanks for the game, boys," he said, pushing back from the table. "I think I'll go grab a bite to eat."

"But you got most of our money," Staples said in a sour voice.

"That's right. My lucky day." Avery got to his feet, and Staples and then Crazy Nick rose with him. Carns sat still, both hands on the table.

"I say we play more cards," Staples said menacingly.

"Go ahead. I'm leavin'."

Staples stepped clear of the table, his hand on his pistol, and Nick followed suit.

Carns, still sitting with his hands in clear sight said evenly, "Let it go Fred."

"Shut up!" Staples snapped, and then glaring at Avery, he said, "Now, Texas, I say we play some cards. Sit back down there."

Avery heard the solitaire player scramble for the door, and suddenly he'd had enough. Crazy Nick was standing too close on his left, and his whiskey-clouded brain was focused as much on Staples as it was on Avery. In one violent motion, Avery lashed out with his left fist, striking him square on the throat with the side of his hand. Nick made a horrible gurgling sound as he collapsed to the floor, and in the split second that Staples's eyes were on Nick, Avery drew his gun. Staples, eyes wide in shock, found himself looking into the barrel of Avery's pistol. Carns hadn't moved.

Avery took a step to his right so he could keep an eye on Nick, who was on his hands and knees making pitiful wheezing sounds. His gun never wavered as, eyes hot and face grim, he said to Staples, "You played stupid; now you're talkin' stupid. Keep it up, and you'll lose more than your money. Now back away from the table."

Fred Staples took a careful step back and, though he hadn't been told to do so, lifted his hands to shoulder height.

"Now, Carns, I figure you for the smart one in the outfit. You stand up slow and keep your hands in sight. You gather up that money there and leave it in a nice pile and then you can back up a step too."

Carns did as he was told, and Avery took a step forward, picked up the money with his left hand, and stuffed it in his pocket. He heard movement behind him.

"Okay, drop the gun, cowboy!"

Avery didn't move.

"You heard me, you saddle tramp," bellowed the voice behind him. "Now drop that gun, or I'll blow your brains all over the wall with this here greener. I'm the law here!"

Still Avery didn't move. His eye's bored into Staples's, the pistol rock steady in his fist. Beads of sweat formed on Staples's forehead as his eyes shifted nervously from Avery to the sheriff.

Then Avery spoke. "How's about you put your gun down, sheriff? You shoot me, and I'll likely blow this gent's brains all over the wall. I ain't done nothin' wrong here, but I still could."

Carns tried to speak, but no sound came. He cleared his throat and tried again. "It's okay, Ernie. Fred invited this stranger here to join our game. He pretty much cleaned us out fair and square. Fred here's had a bit too much liquor, and he was a sore loser. Him an' Crazy Nick made to jump this fella, and it didn't go too good for 'em."

Adam Carns's voice of reason cut through Avery's anger, and he took a step back and slowly lowered and then holstered his pistol. Relief washed over Staples's face as he dropped his hands, keeping them well away from his gun. Avery turned to regard Carns for a brief moment, and their eyes met. Then he turned slowly to face the sheriff, who still had his shotgun trained on him.

"I said to drop your gun, mister."

"So you did."

Douglas Rawling

"Get your horse and get on out of here."

"When I'm ready." Still covered by the sheriff's gun, Avery turned and walked slowly from the room.

CHAPTER THREE

Back on the street, Avery was again at a loss for what to do. It would soon be supper time, but he had no desire to face the pretty waitress at the hotel; in fact, he had no desire to face anyone. The tension from the last few minutes left him feeling wound up and irritable. He knew he'd been provoked, but it troubled him that he'd come close to taking another man's life over something so trivial. He wondered if placing little value on your own life couldn't cause you to see other's lives in the same light.

He decided to cross the street to the mercantile, make his purchases, and then go get his horses and pick the supplies up on his way out of town. He'd have enough daylight left to make camp somewhere up river. He remembered then that he'd checked in at the hotel, but again, because he didn't want to face the woman in the gray dress, he decided to just forget about it. If he didn't show up, they'd soon figure it out, and because he hadn't stayed there, he wouldn't owe them anything. It struck him as ironic that, like a self-fulfilling prophecy, his self-imposed exile was now being forced on him. He'd ridden into town thinking he wanted no part of these people, and now they wanted no part of him.

What had the sheriff called him? A saddle tramp. Back home, he'd always been a somebody. He had a known history that went with him everywhere. Here he was nobody. Well, wasn't that what he'd wanted? Wasn't that why he hadn't gone back?

The first thing he saw when he stepped into the mercantile was a small boy about five years old looking longingly at a display of pocketknives. His bib overalls were patched and patched again, but they were clean, and his hair was combed down flat. Behind the counter, watching him like a hawk was the red-haired man from the restaurant. As Avery was about to walk by, the boy pointed to a knife with an ivory inlay of an elk set in a red handle and asked, "How much does this one cost, Mr. McFadden?"

"It's expensive," came the condescending reply.

"Yes, sir."

Avery took a second look at the man behind the counter and felt the urge to punch him in the mouth. He shook his head and smiled to himself. *Why not?* he thought. *I could really endear myself to the citizens of Bow City.* He was just turning to walk down the rear aisle while taking his eyes from the scene at the counter, when his shoulder collided heavily with someone coming the other way. He turned to see the woman from the restaurant stagger backward, gasping in pain and surprise as the stack of fabric she'd been carrying fell to the floor.

Avery looked into her startled blue eyes and said quickly, "Sorry, ma'am, I didn't see you." He stooped to pick the dress material off the floor, and as he straightened to hand it back to her, he asked clumsily, "Are you all right?"

"I'm okay," she responded, biting her bottom lip and not meeting his gaze. "I didn't see you either." They both stood awkwardly for a moment, and then the woman said, "If you'll excuse me."

Avery stepped aside, and she walked past him to the counter. His eyes followed her a moment, and then he turned and made his way down the aisle and past the dress goods to where he saw some heavy, sheepskin-lined leather coats.

As he took one down to try it on, the woman from the restaurant came back down the aisle toward him. He was very aware of her presence, but she seemed unaware of his. He glanced her way and couldn't help but notice the similarities between her, as she admired a bolt of silky green cloth, and the boy he'd seen looking at the knives by the counter. He was suddenly conscious of the poker money that bulged in his pocket, but with the coat under his arm, he retreated around the end of the aisle and headed for the canned goods. When he brought his things to the counter, he was just in time to see the woman leaving with the boy.

"Filthy little tramp."

"What's that?" Avery asked, turning to face the man

behind the counter, who gestured with a nod toward the door.

"I'd just as soon not serve her kind in here."

Avery didn't answer, but the look on his face showed he was confused.

"Mrs. Harper. She claims she's the widow of an army officer. Me, I know better."

"How's that?"

With a sly, knowing look in his little, green eyes, the man the boy had called McFadden said, "I seen her in Denver a coupla times dealin' faro at the High Roller Casino. She wasn't wearin' near so many clothes then. She's a gambler—a gambler and a whore."

Avery didn't know if what McFadden said was true or not. He did know, however, that he was quickly developing a profound dislike for the man. "Could be," Avery said noncommittally. "I noticed in the restaurant today that you don't mind lookin' at her though."

McFadden threw back his head in a raucous laugh. "There is that," he said agreeably. "Just don't be tellin' the Mrs."

👁 👁

No one was at the barn, so Avery headed out back and caught his horses. The light was beginning to fade, so he decided he'd saddle up outside where it was easier to see, even though it meant packing his things from inside. As he threw his saddle on his horse, he noticed that the owner of the barn had begun to expand his corrals, and several new posts were set in and a few rails lay scattered around. He was tightening the diamond on his packhorse when the hostler stepped through the back door of the barn.

"Sorry, I never seen you come in. I was just grabbin' a bite over at the hotel."

"That's fine. I've saddled my own horse a time or two," Avery said.

"Heard about the little set-to over at the saloon," the hostler said. "I wouldn't worry too much about Sheriff Coleman if I was you. You're welcome to throw your bedroll down in the loft if you like."

"Thanks. I think I'll drift. How much do I owe you?"

Wally waved a hand to dismiss the question. "Nothin'. I never even got around to forkin' hay to them ponies. Are you sure you want to be travelin'? There's nothin' close by but wild country, and it's late to be ridin'.'"

"I've been seein' a lotta wild country lately. It suites me fine."

The hostler glanced to the west where the sun was sinking to the mountains, looked back to Avery, and asked, "You goin' up river or down?"

His friendly attitude seemed genuine, so Avery answered, "I think I'll head west."

"The Double Diamond's up that way. If you're set on campin' out though, there's a feeder creek comes in from the north about four miles up. Nice little aspen stand with plenty of fire wood and shelter should the wind pick up. Camp there myself sometimes. It's my favorite fishin' hole."

The man's friendliness was a balm to Avery's nerves. He silently wondered at it, for he'd done nothing to deserve it. After tying off the lash cinch, he turned and offered the man his hand. "Avery Carson. Recently of Texas."

"Wally Gibbs. You'll most likely be ridin' back through in a week or so, 'cause there's nothing much west of here, and winter's comin'. Stop in and I'll buy you a meal."

"Thanks, but I don't reckon I'll be back. I may just cut across that ridge and follow the range north for a bit. I've heard there's good cow country up that way."

"Good cow country right here if that's what you're lookin' for."

Avery wasn't sure why he said it. It just came out easy and natural. "I ain't sure what I'm lookin' for."

"Figured as much."

The men shared a few moments of comfortable silence, and when Avery swung into the saddle, he remembered his hotel key. Standing in the stirrups, he dug in his pocket and said, "Say, Wally, I almost forgot, I got a key from the hotel. You wouldn't mind droppin' it off next time you're in there, would you?"

Wally reached up and took the key. "I can do that," he said. "Ride safe."

"Thanks."

Avery rode around the east end of the barn and took the street west. He found Wally Gibb's campsite with no problem, and it was a good place to spend the night. About forty yards upstream from where the feeder creek flowed into the river, it tumbled through a notch in the rocks and over a small falls, spilling into a wide pool. Avery could see several good-sized trout lying in the deep, cold water, and it made him wish he had a fishing pole. He off saddled and unpacked, picketed his horses, and built his fire at the foot of the aspens.

His head came up sharply as a shrill, piercing sound split the cool fall air, and he realized it must be an elk bugling. It was the first time he'd heard the haunting, forlorn sound, and it stirred something deep within his soul. Later, under a canopy of stars, he watched his fire while nursing a hot cup of coffee. He felt a quiet peace he couldn't explain, and he thought it strange considering the events of the day. The fire was a circle of glowing coals when he rose to his feet, threw out the dregs from his cup, and went to his bedroll.

The next morning dawned dull and gray. The temperature had dropped several degrees and Avery was glad for his new coat. Instead of taking the trail by the river, he followed the feeder creek up a gentle slope through slender pines. Eventually the banks became steep and choked with deadfall, and he was forced to choose his own way. He was well above the valley floor, and in the distance could see a clutter of buildings he guessed would be home to the Double Diamond. Today he was content with solitude, and he was eager to get through the pass to the west.

A couple of hours later, well beyond the Double Diamond, he dropped down to the valley where travel was easier. He followed the river west, and when the slopes along the north bank grew steep, he splashed across a wide gravelly bar and then scrambled up the bank on the opposite side. For a while, he rode through rolling grassland, but then the hills to the south began closing in, and the path he followed became little more than a game trail. The sound of the river was now a constant roar as it foamed and crashed down its steep and narrow course. Looking ahead, it was hard to see where the pass would be, as the way seemed barred by a solid wall of cold, gray rock. The trail persisted however, and the river had found a way, so Avery continued the steady climb, pausing every so often to let his horses catch their wind.

The country began to level off, and he found himself on a short, grassy meadow that ended abruptly at the foot of a boulder-strewn hillside. Here the river took a hard bend to the south between two overlapping sandstone cliffs, disappearing behind the ridge in front of him. The game trail was well used, and he followed it through the notch above the river, the mountains rising steeply on either side, standing guard on a narrow valley that seldom saw the sun.

It was almost a surprise and relief when he broke free of the pass. He reined his horse in, captured by the vista that stretched out before him. Straight ahead was a wide valley of grass that gradually climbed to broken, pine-covered hills about five miles in the distance. Behind the hills rose a majestic, snow-covered range that dwarfed the one he'd just come through. About half a mile out on the valley floor, the river broke off into two branches, one angling in from the northwest and the other from the southwest. What he realized almost at once, was that he was looking across the width of the valley, not its breadth. It seemed to run roughly north and south between the two mountain ranges and was lost from sight behind the shoulders of the mountains in both directions. This was a big and beautiful country, and it owned him from the moment he saw it.

It was late afternoon, and he decided to camp right where he was. Tomorrow, he'd ford the river and explore the north fork. Stepping down from his horse, he said aloud, "I think this might be home."

CHAPTER FOUR

Avery spent two days following the northwest branch. The first day's ride took him through what looked like good grazing land, though he wasn't sure how deep the snow would pile in during the winter. On the second day, the valley grew narrow; the ground became swampy and, in places, was clogged with small spruce. The following morning, he decided to head cross-country on his way back south. At some point, he'd pick up the south fork of the river and follow it back to his camp near the pass. Wanting to see as much country as possible, he hugged the hills on the west side of the valley.

Snow fell off and on for the next two days, though never amounting to more than an inch or two on the ground. The third morning on his trip south, he broke camp to a clear, blue sky with a warm west breeze blowing.

It was late afternoon when Avery spotted a herd of elk lying on a side hill. Thinking it would be good to have camp meat, he tied his horses out of sight in a timbered draw, pulled his rifle from the scabbard, and began working his way along the slope. When he reached the top of the ridge, he had a good view of the elk about 150 yards away and on an opposing slope. Thumbing back the hammer on his Winchester, he was just drawing a bead on a young bull when one of the cows stood up, her attention fixed on something in the valley to the east. More elk got to their feet, and the whole herd had their heads up, looking off in the same direction. Avery followed their line of sight, and quickly shrunk back behind a tree.

Out on the flat, seven Indians were riding single file, and though he had no idea what tribe they were from, they were well armed and looked like trouble. Avery had a sinking feeling, remembering the clear trail he'd left in the melting snow. The way the Indians were traveling, they'd come upon it in a matter of minutes. In a crouching run, he made his way back to his horses and slammed his rifle back into the scabbard. He hit the saddle, moving out in an awkward stop-and-go trot, winding through the timber and trying to keep his packhorse on the right side of the trees. He crossed over the ridge, hoping to keep it between himself and the Indians, so that when he made the grassland he could take off at a hard run, unseen.

Movement up the slope and to his right caught his attention, and he turned to see a single mounted Indian, buck jumping down the hill through the deadfall toward him. Avery hit the flats running hard, and the big-boned packhorse couldn't keep up, so he let him go. His gelding was stretching out now, and because the warrior coming off the slopes had to angle to cut him off, Avery was gaining. He glanced over his shoulder and saw that the Indian, realizing he was losing the horserace, was lining up with his rifle. Avery hunched forward in the saddle, his face in the horse's mane, and hoped for the best.

He felt his horse take the bullet a fraction of a second before he heard the blast from the rifle and was able to kick his feet free of the stirrups as the gelding folded up, tumbling forward in a wild summersault. Avery was thrown clear, but he hit the ground hard, rolling over several times before coming to a stop, his breath driven from his lungs. Gasping for air, he got to his knees and saw that the Indian's pony, spooked by the rifle shot, was pitching violently. The warrior had a fist full of mane and was doing his best to stay with the horse. He lost the battle and was slammed face-first down into the tall grass. When he got to his feet, Avery saw that he still held his rifle.

The distance was too great for a pistol shot, so laboring for breath, Avery staggered back to his dying horse to get his Winchester. The horse was lying on it, and only a shattered stock was visible. A shot sounded behind him, and in desperation, Avery frantically pulled at the rifle, trying to get it free. It was hopeless. He glanced over his shoulder and then threw himself to the ground as the Indian, who had closed the distance, let go another shot. Avery heard the bullet sing past his ear, and oblivious of the thrashing hooves, dove for cover behind his convulsing horse. He drew his pistol and, rising up on one knee, let go three fast shots. The running Indian stopped dead, dropped back to a sitting position, and then fell slowly to the side, rolling over on his face.

Still fighting for air, Avery turned and looked behind him. About half a mile back, the other Indians had just rounded the shoulder of the hill and were coming on hard. He looked back the other way and saw the steep cut banks of the south fork about fifty yards ahead. He holstered his pistol and, in a clumsy, stumbling run, covered the distance in what seemed like forever.

He could hear the pounding of hooves as he reached the bank, and without hesitation, he jumped in. The cold water hit him like a hammer, and sharp pain split through his head, but he let the current take him, staying under as long as he could stand. When he surfaced, he was drifting swiftly past some overhanging willows where the current had undercut the bank. With arms like lead and no feeling in his hands, he grasped at the branches, pulling himself up and out of the water. He then clawed his way into the dark shelter of the overhang. Overhead was a ceiling of sod and a thick tangle of roots and branches. He had no idea if his feet were visible, and he drew his knees up close to his chest, both in an attempt to hide, and in an effort to fight off the intense cold. He could see nothing and, shaking violently, could not keep his teeth from chattering. He heard voices and tried to suck himself into a smaller ball. Then all was quiet.

He wanted to live. Not long ago, he would have debated that point, but today, when there'd been a chance to die, he'd fought desperately to live. Strangely, the thought was a comfort to him. At least he knew the truth.

Again he heard voices, this time raised in argument. They faded away up stream, and left behind only the sound of running water. He knew he'd never warm up unless he was moving, and he knew that once darkness fell, he'd have to take a chance and leave his hideaway. He didn't think he'd survive the night where he was, especially as the temperature would be dropping. He was glad that evening wasn't far off; even so, the daylight seemed to want to hang on forever.

When it was almost dark he began to test his legs, straightening them and then drawing them back. He did it once and stopped to listen. He did it again and then again and again. He felt the blood begin to flow, and he moved his arms what little he could while he clenched and unclenched his fists. He hoped the darkness of his hole wasn't deceiving him, but he felt sure it must be time, and he began slowly to worm his way feet-first out into the open. He reached up and gripped the willows while digging his heels into the bank to keep from falling back into the icy water. Teetering a moment, his legs clumsy and unresponsive, he threw an arm over some branches and managed to stay upright. He stood that way for a while, stiff and exhausted, and then, with great effort, was able to drag himself up and over the bank.

Immediately he shrunk down, face against the ground, afraid to move. Across the river where his horse lay, a fire was burning. Every now and then, someone would move between himself and the flames, and Avery was sure the light would show him up. Cautiously, he crawled away to the deeper darkness; got to his feet; and, on unsteady legs, began walking downstream. When he'd gone a short distance, he paused to reload his pistol and then struck out again. He traveled through the night, and eventually, his clothing began to dry out and warmth returned to his body. He'd lost his hat when he'd jumped into the river, and his clothes were caked with mud.

As gray dawn began to build in the east, he started looking for a place to hide. The riverbank had worked before, so he focused his attention there. He found a similar spot under some willows and was about to lower himself down when his head came up sharply. He paused to listen. He could have sworn he'd heard the sound of distant gunfire, but now, there was nothing but the wind. He waited a few moments more and then, doing his best not to disturb the soil, crawled into his shelter. Exhausted, he slept.

He woke in the early afternoon, thirsty and hungry. He knew he should just stay where he was, for if he climbed down the bank to drink, he'd leave telltale marks in the mud. He decided to tough it out and wait till dark. Time dragged on, and the sound of running water so close by when he had an overpowering thirst, was more than he could stand. Throwing caution to the wind, he crawled out from his hideaway and down to the water's edge, where he drank deep and long. His thirst satisfied, he straightened up, turned, and saw where his boots had skidded down the bank. Breaking off a willow branch, he wiped out the marks as well as he could. He then backed away from the soft earth by the water's edge, wiping out his tracks there as well. Throwing the branch in the river, he cautiously raised his head and peered over the top of the bank.

Nothing moved on the long, wide valley floor but the brown, swaying grass. Slowly, he raised his head a little farther for a better look. The landscape as far as the eye could see was empty. He noticed the river was winding northeast and was surprised that he was little more than halfway across the valley. He guessed that, because he'd stuck close to the meandering river during the night, he hadn't covered much distance as the crow flies. This concerned him, but it felt good to be able to move around and stretch his legs. Instead of crawling back under the bank, he decided to sit and wait where he was. He could take a look every so often, and he should be able to see anyone coming a long ways off.

The sun crept toward the western horizon, and there was still no movement out on the tall grass. An impatience to be moving, spurred on by a gnawing hunger, caused him to grow restless. With the day's fading light still falling on a silent, lonely world, Avery climbed the bank, stood up straight, and looked around. He was alone. He could see the notch in the mountains in the distance and, remembering the food he'd stashed at his campsite, boldly struck out, wanting to make the most of what little light he had left. Ahead, the river bent sharply to the north, only to double back on itself about a half mile farther on. Instead of following the river, Avery cut straight across the open ground, wanting to save time and distance.

They came like ghosts up out of a fold on the valley floor. Avery heard hooves whisper in the grass and spun around to face five stone-faced warriors riding slowly toward him. They fanned out a short distance off, drew to a stop, and watched him, lances pointing at the sky. Avery had nowhere to run. He stood silent where he was, the setting sun on his face and the west wind moving his hair. Slowly, he dropped his right hand the short distance it took to remove the leather thong from the hammer of his pistol and then he waited. The warrior in the center handed his rifle to the man next to him and then moved away from the others. He stopped and drove his lance into the ground before coming slowly forward again. As he approached, Avery noticed fresh scalps hanging from his horse's mane, and realized for the first time that the man was leading his packhorse.

The Indian pulled up about twenty feet away, placed the palm of his right hand on his chest, tapped it three times and said, "Shoshoni." He then turned and motioned with his arm to the north and said again, "Shoshoni." Then he motioned west and south, saying again, "Shoshoni." Next, he raised a fist and then brought it down in a sweeping motion, opening his hand as he did so. "Cheyenne bad," he said. Again he raised a fist and made the same downward motion. "We kill." He then pointed at Avery. "Fight good," he said. Pointing his finger like a pistol, he made three shooting motions, saying, "Boom, boom, boom," and then, holding up three fingers, he tapped them hard three times on his chest. "Fight good," he repeated. Riding slowly toward Avery, he dropped the lead shank of the packhorse, stopped, and pointed skyward with his left hand. Reaching across with his right, he gripped the raised finger and said, "Keep."

Without another word, he turned and rode away. The other warriors fell in behind, and it was then that Avery noticed his packhorse had no saddle and the Indian in the rear was riding his.

CHAPTER FIVE

Avery glanced over his shoulder at the retreating Indians and couldn't believe his luck. Apparently, this was Shoshoni hunting grounds, and if these braves were any indication, the Shoshoni's were friendly to the whites. Maybe it was because he'd killed one of their enemies, but for some reason, they'd taken a notion, sought him out, and returned his horse. The fact that he was riding bareback with only a halter shank to guide the gelding did not lessen the fact that he felt both relieved and thankful.

It soon became obvious why the horse was a packhorse, however, and not a saddle horse. He had big, feathered feet and a gait that seemed to have as much side to side swing as it did forward motion. Avery was grateful, though, that his back was well rounded and not all that uncomfortable to ride. He managed to get the horse into a heavy trot and kept it up while the evening gave way to darkness.

Ahead of him, a horse whinnied and Avery's heart jumped in his chest. He tried to pull his horse in, but it stubbornly leaned into the halter and, to Avery's dismay, gave an answering whiny. He strong-armed the gelding into a circle and managed to get him stopped, but he knew it was too late. He strained to see what was ahead, his horse tossing its head against the pressure on the halter. Avery could hear no sound of approaching riders, and maybe whoever was out there was as cautious as he was.

Drawing his pistol, he let the horse walk slowly forward and then pulled him in again as another whiny came out of the darkness. Then straight ahead, lying low against a backdrop of aspens, Avery could swear he saw the roofline of a building. Again the other horse whinnied, and Avery moved cautiously forward. Presently, the outline of one building and then another showed up dimly in the gloom. Avery let the horse have its head, and it walked eagerly forward. He rode into a yard that, except for a lone horse running back and forth behind a rail fence, was as still as death.

"Hello, the house!" he called.

The horse stopped its pacing and nickered softly.

"Hello, the house!" he called again, only this time a bit louder.

Nothing.

Sliding to the ground, Avery walked up to the cabin door and knocked tentatively. He waited and then knocked more loudly. Feeling for the handle, he opened the door and stuck his head inside. "Anybody home?"

All was still. By the dim light over the western mountains, Avery could see a hitching rail to the side of the cabin door. He tied his horse and stepped hesitantly inside. Instinctively feeling down the side of the door, he found a tin can nailed to the wall. It was full of matches. He struck one and, by its light, saw a coal oil lamp on a dust-covered table just to the right of the door. He lifted the chimney, lit the wick, and a warm, soft light transformed the room.

He was standing at the end wall of a log cabin that was about twice as long as it was wide. It had no ceiling, and three log beams running lengthwise supported the roof. The back of the cabin was walled off by a partition with a curtained-off door to what he presumed would be a bedroom. The place was surprisingly well furnished with a small table and chairs, a wood cookstove, and two leather chairs that faced each other from opposing corners. On the floor between them was a heavy bearskin rug.

The room smelled stale and close, everything was covered in dust, and he was sure no one had been there for quite some time. Taking the lamp from the table, he crossed the floor and hesitantly pushed back the curtain. No one was in the room, the bed was neatly made, and hanging in orderly fashion on the back wall was an assortment of clothing. Across the room from the bed, beneath a small mirror, was a dresser with a tin washbasin. It too was covered in dust.

Setting the lamp back on the table, Avery went outside and led his gelding to a rail gate where the lone horse waited, neck arched and nickering eagerly. He turned his horse loose, and the two ponies thundered off into the night, kicking and squealing.

Back in the cabin, he found several tins of tomatoes

and beans and, finding a can opener by the stove, wolfed down one can of each. He drank the juice from the tomato can, wiped his chin with the back of his hand, and then headed for the bedroom and pulled a blanket from the bed. After blowing out the lamp, he stretched out on the bearskin rug and was soon asleep.

He woke early the next morning, eager to have a look around. The warm weather had held through the night, and the sky was promising a beautiful day. Three buildings—the house, a barn, and a storage shed—stood in the yard. All were built of logs squared with a broad ax and made with tight-fitting dovetailed corners. The buildings sat in the Y formed by the river and an energetic creek that flowed through an aspen grove after tumbling down the slope behind the cabin. About a hundred yards on either side of the creek, the hills behind the cabin rose steeply, forming a canyon of sorts. The gate he'd put his horse through last night was next to the barn and part of a rail fence that made a half circle running from one canyon slope to the other. He could see the horses grazing halfway up the draw, and beyond that, it looked like there was a little hanging valley. Behind the valley towered the imposing main range of mountains. It was a beautiful spot, and he wondered who and where the owner was.

He could see a set of corrals behind the barn, and decided to investigate. Instead of opening the gate, he climbed over the rail fence, and as he did, something caught his eye. Wedged between the gatepost and the bottom rail was a sun-faded black Stetson, and soil had drifted over the brim so that it was partially buried.

Avery stooped to pick it up, a soft, steady breeze blowing from the southwest. He walked slowly toward the corral, the wind in his face, and then he stopped short. There, beneath the bottom rail, half in the corral, half out, lay the decomposed body of a man.

Avery walked hesitantly forward, his attention fixed on the ghastly scene before him. Then a third time he was brought up short. Lying almost in the center of the corral was the remains of a horse, its head twisted skyward in an awkward angle. It was held that way by a stout rope tied to a metal ring on a snubbing post, and the sun-dried hulk of a saddle lay in the dirt not far off. Turning from the scene in the corral, he walked forward to kneel down beside the dead man. For some reason, the wild animals had left both bodies alone, and maybe it was because they were so close to the buildings. The birds, however, had picked at the bones, and through a torn and tattered shirt, Avery could see the man's ribs on his right side had been caved in. His left foot was turned oddly and pointing in entirely the wrong direction.

The story was as clear as if Avery had witnessed it. The man had been attempting to saddle a colt. He would have been careful to stay clear of the hind feet, and Avery knew this because he'd been through it himself many times. The horse had lashed out with a front hoof, breaking the man's leg. He'd gone down, and the bronc had stomped on him. The man most likely would've died regardless, but because no one else was around, the horse had killed himself too.

Avery turned his back on the scene and sat down,

leaning against the corral. The senselessness of the tragedy seemed to tumble in on him. It spoke like a far-off voice to the deepest part of his being, trying to tell him something that he couldn't quite hear. Avery had no idea why, but for the first time since his wife's death, in fact for the first time since he was a child, he wept. After a time, he lifted his face from the cradle of his hands, staring off at nothing. He turned and looked into the hollow eye sockets of the man beside him, and he knew that he was alone.

"Everyone needs somebody," he told the man. He stood up, and was then aware he was still holding the man's hat. He beat it against his leg, knocking away the dirt and then pulled it down on his head firmly and deliberately as if making a statement. The hat fit perfectly, and it was a good hat.

Avery spent the rest of the day dealing with the bodies of the man and the horse. First, he made a wide circle around the property to see if there were any other graves. Finding none, he took a pick and a shovel from the storage shed and dug a hole on a shaded knoll between the aspens and the mountains. It was a pretty spot with a good view to the north, and shelter from the wind. For a reason he did not entirely understand, it seemed important to do the job well, and though the ground was rocky beneath the topsoil, he dug the grave three feet wide and six feet deep. He found a large stack of planks in the barn, and he used one to make a cross that he drove into the ground at the head of the grave. There was no name on the cross, but he made himself a promise to do what he could to find it out and carve it in later. Next, he grabbed a blanket from the house, went to the corral, and gingerly pulled the corpse from under the rail. He was relieved when the bones held together, and he wrapped the dead man in the blanket and carried him to the open grave. Laying the body gently by the hole, he jumped in and then carefully lowered the man to his final resting place.

He climbed back out; picked up the shovel; and with slow, deliberate movements, filled in the grave. The task complete, he set the shovel aside, removed his hat, and at first was at a loss for what to say. Then he prayed.

"Lord, it ain't a good thing to die alone. I don't know why you let it happen. I don't know a lotta things. I don't know why my wife had to die. I don't know why my little baby never got born. I guess it's partly 'cause I'm a stubborn, stupid man."

He paused for a while, deep in thought, and then continued, "The preacher says you are with us always, so I guess you were here when this happened. I guess you know this fella's name. I know he was a good builder and liked wild and beautiful places. I know he liked things neat and orderly. I don't know why he chose to live way out here so far from other folks. Maybe he was driven to it; maybe it was his choice. I know I seen a Bible in the cabin when I was fetchin' the blanket, so I'm guessin' he was a man that talked to you from time to time. I guess that's all I got to say right now. I'll leave him in your care. Amen."

Avery replaced his hat and then turned and walked soberly back through the aspens to the barn. He was wondering how he was going to drag the dead horse out of the corral, as he needed a saddle, and his was on some Indian pony somewhere. The one in the corral was badly weathered and may not hold together. He went into the barn, and after a brief search found some neat's-foot oil. Throwing the saddle over a rail, he spent a good hour working life back into the dry, cracked leather. The cinch was also a real concern, as some animal had chewed through over half the cords. He knew there wouldn't be much weight left in the horse's carcass though, so he figured it should still be strong enough. Next, he picked up his halter and climbed the hill to catch a horse.

He had his first real look at the dead man's saddle horse, and he liked what he saw. He was a solid-looking, short-coupled buckskin with a big hip and a good eye. Judging by the age and the scald marks on the withers, Avery figured he would be well broke. The horse was branded CP on the left hip and had an unusual white splash right below the brand that looked not unlike angel wings. Avery slipped a halter on the horse and wondered if the brand might provide some clue as to the owner's name.

Back at the barn, Avery saddled the horse, took a rope from an empty saddle rack, and headed for the corral. The gelding shied and snorted at the carcass but soon settled down, and Avery was able to lead him close enough so he could strip off the halter. He tried to untie the shank, but it was pulled tight on the metal ring. With his saddle horse threatening to bolt, he figured it would be best to leave it for later. Putting a loop around the dead animal's back legs, he mounted up and took a couple of dallies.

The frayed cinch held while he dragged the carcass a few hundred yards out onto the grass. He left it there for the coyotes and the magpies.

∽∽   ∽∽

A warm, Indian summer evening slowly faded to night. Avery sat on a polished stump chair in front of the cabin, listening to the wind and the running creek. His coffee cup was empty and had been for some time, but he stayed where he was. Earlier, he'd found a trapdoor under the bearskin rug that led to a cool room beneath the cabin. It was well stocked with food, and he'd helped himself, enjoying a supper of smoked ham, pan bread, and beans. He'd also found a small dam behind the cabin with a water pipe pointing downstream where it spouted clear, cold water. The pipe was supported by a stout metal tripod about three feet above the creek bed, and just below the tripod, two squared timbers spanned the creek, forming a level platform to stand on while you filled your bucket.

Though Avery had never met the man who'd built the place, he knew he liked him. He had a deep feeling of doing something right in finding his remains and burying them before time could completely erase the memory of him. He was going to stay here, and he felt right about that too. He would try to find the man's relatives, and if they were to inherit, he'd offer to pay for the place. If they wanted to move in, well he'd deal with that when the time came. For now, though, this would be home.

He'd also been doing some thinking in other areas.

The day the man and the horse had had their showdown, they'd both thought they were doing the right thing, and it had gotten them both killed. He struggled to wrap his thoughts around why the implications of this seemed so important. Maybe it was because he'd always been a man so sure of himself. He'd willingly been the sometimes "brutal hand of the law" while riding with the Texas Rangers, because he knew what was right. Now he was remembering two brothers who had squatted on a creek coveted by a couple of big ranchers. The ranchers had reported missing cattle, and who else was there to blame? Avery and two other Rangers had ridden up to the men's shack. They had resisted arrest, and in the gun battle that ensued, both had been killed. Within a week, the shack had been burned to the ground, and one of the big rancher's cattle were grazing the surrounding hills. Avery wondered now if there had even been any missing cattle. He got wearily to his feet, sighed heavily, and stepped inside.

He decided to spend the night on the bearskin rug again. He knew in time he'd become more comfortable living in the cabin, but for now he still had the feeling of trespassing. As he spread his blankets, he remembered the dead man's Bible. It occurred to him that the man's name might be written inside, so he went to the bedroom and brought it out to the lamp on the table.

The Bible was old and well used, and he opened it with care. Sure enough, on the inside cover was a handwritten note.

My dearest Clancy,

May God protect you while you are in far-off India. I am giving you your father's Bible, which he gave to me shortly before his death. I am so sorry that you never knew him. He was a fine man and a brave soldier. He would have been so proud of you. It came to me last night while you were in my prayers that, if you want to know your father, first look at yourself and then secondly, and perhaps more importantly, read the verses underlined by his hand. It will help you to know his heart.

I will love you always, and if by chance my Lord calls me home before your return, we will meet again, and your father and I shall greet you.

Love your mother,
Emily
Philippians 1:21.

Avery closed the Bible and set it gently on the table. A moment later, he picked it up again, reread the note inside the cover, and then fumbled through the pages till he found Philippians 1:21. It read, "For me to live is Christ, and to die is gain."

He read and reread it, his brow furrowed. He figured he knew what "to die is gain" meant, but he wasn't sure about the first part. Down the page a little ways another verse was underlined. He read, "For I am in a strait betwixt two, having a desire to depart, and to be with

Christ; which is far better: Nevertheless to abide in the flesh is more needful for you."

Avery closed the Bible again and set it on the table. He knew he wanted to stay alive, but he was pretty sure it was for his own account, and he didn't know what to make of what he'd just read. At least he knew the man he'd buried was named Clancy. Judging by the brand on his horse, his last name likely started with a P. Avery blew out the lamp and went to his blankets.

Sleep was slow in coming, as restless thoughts refused to leave his mind alone. He remembered the last verse he'd read, and he wondered if he'd ever truly done anything on someone else's account. He realized he liked the respect others had paid him back in Texas, and he'd felt pressure to live up to expectations placed on him. He'd believed he'd been building up the ranch for Audrey and the children they'd have, and this was partly the truth. He realized it was also largely true that, behind it all, he was a proud man and had wanted to succeed. He'd been doing it for Avery. If he hadn't been so busy with "important things" that morning, he'd have remembered Audrey had a doctor's appointment, and he would have made sure the old team was home. He should have driven her to town. That was what she'd been silently asking for when she'd said she was afraid to drive the grays. He also realized that, though he thought he'd left everything behind, nothing had really changed. Self-pity was just another form of selfish pride. He remembered the dead horse hanging from the hitching post, and he said aloud, "That'll be me if I ain't careful."

A vision of the little boy staring at the display of knives came to his mind, and he was suddenly impatient to go back to Bow City. He'd be needing to go there anyway to load up on supplies for the coming winter, and he figured he should report the death of Clancy to the sheriff. He'd most likely met the man and may know how to contact his next of kin.

With a new sense of purpose for the coming day, Avery turned on his side and pulled the blankets up over his shoulders. A short time later, he was asleep.

CHAPTER SIX

Before heading for town, Avery did a quick inventory of what he had for supplies. In the bedroom, he found a Henry rifle and a new Colt revolver with an ivory pistol grip. He spun the cylinder and felt the weight of it with experienced hands and then snapped it up and sighted down the barrel. It was a fine weapon, but he decided he liked the familiar feel of his old, walnut-handled Colt, so he hung the newer one on the bed post. He looked down at his jeans, still soiled from his nights on the river and, on impulse, took off his shirt and tried on one of the clean ones hanging on the wall. It fit perfectly. Next, he kicked off his boots, unbuckled his shell belt, stepped out of his jeans, and put on a clean pair. They fit perfectly as well.

"Well I'll be," he said aloud. Going to the stove, he took his money from the warming oven where he'd spread it out to dry and stuffed it in his pocket. Shrugging into his coat, he stepped outside to catch the horses. Half an hour later, he was on his way to Bow City.

He passed his camp at the gap but knew he'd have to wait till he had a packsaddle before he could move his stashed supplies. He paid close attention to the trail through the pass, as he'd been wondering how Clancy had managed to pack a cookstove to his building sight. He'd thought the trail too narrow for a wagon but now was thinking it maybe could be done. He stopped several times to push boulders from the trail, sending them crashing down to the river below and guessed they'd tumbled down onto the trail since the time Clancy had moved in. Because he stuck to the valley floor, he made much better time than he had when leaving Bow City, and three hours after riding through the gap, he passed the Double Diamond buildings. Less than two hours later, he rode into town.

Wally Gibbs was out back working on the corrals when Avery dismounted in front of the livery barn. He led his horses down the alley, tied them in an empty stall, and stepped out through the double doors at the back of the barn. Wally looked up from his work, a surprised smile on his face.

"Didn't expect you back quite so soon," he said.

"That was a fine campsite. Thanks."

"You found it all right?"

Avery nodded.

"See any big ol' trout lyin' in that hole beneath the falls?"

"I did. Made me wish I was a kid."

"You don't have to be a kid to go fishin'," Wally said,

wiping his hands clean on an old rag. "If you did, it wouldn't be worth growin' up."

Avery smiled, and he wished as he often did that words came more easily to him. He liked this friendly man, and to him, that was not a small thing.

"It's a bit early for supper," Wally said, "but I promised you a meal when you made town. How about it?"

"Well, I could eat; that's for sure," Avery said. "You don't have to get mine though. I still got my poker money."

Wally laughed. "I guess you do," he said. "You can get mine next time." Wally threw his rag aside and made to leave, but Avery stopped him.

"Just a moment Wally," he said. "I'd like to ask you some questions first."

"Sure," Wally said, a curious look on his face. "Fire away."

Avery shuffled his weight from one foot to another, not quite knowing where to begin. Then he said, "I suppose you could use a little help skiddin' some rails down from them hills."

Wally nodded, his face puzzled. "Sure," he said, "but I couldn't pay."

Avery waved his hand as if brushing at a bothersome fly. "No, no," he said. "I was just wonderin' if I could help."

"Sure, and thanks. It would be nice to finish before winter sets in."

Avery nodded and looked pleased. Then he continued.

"Would you mind if I hired a young fella to help peel them rails?"

Wally looked startled. "Why should you hire someone when I ain't even payin' you myself?" he asked.

Again Avery brushed away an unseen fly. "It wouldn't be much," he said. "It's just, when I was leavin' town, I seen this kid in the mercantile admirin' some pocketknives. He asked the store owner what they was worth, and the store owner brushed him off like he was some mangy, old stray dog. I didn't like it. Then when the boy left with his ma, the store owner said some unkind things about her. Even if it was true, I didn't like it either."

Wally nodded slowly. "McFadden. A sanctimonious blister," he said.

Avery nodded. "That would be him all right. Is that true? What he said about the boy's ma? She's the lady waitin' tables at the restaurant."

Wally shrugged and said, "Could be. I wouldn't know. McFadden's done his best to make sure everyone in town knows about it though."

Avery remembered the girl's guarded manner when he'd first met her and realized what she must have been thinking when he'd appeared to be unfriendly, and it troubled him.

"Are they buyin' the story? The town folks, I mean."

"For the most part, I'd say. I don't think she's had an easy time of it."

Avery shook his head, looking down at his feet. "Anyway," he continued, "about the boy ..."

"Peter, Peter Harper," Wally interjected.

Avery looked at him and nodded. "I figure it might appear odd for a stranger to just up an' buy him a pocketknife, so I figured to hire him to peel some rails. I'd ask him if he's got a good knife, and when he says no, I'd give him some money and send him over to the store to pick one out. I'd tell him the knife would be part of his pay and to make sure he bought a good one 'cause I don't want no lazy kid slackin' off and not doin' a good job on accounta he ain't got a good knife."

Wally studied Avery's face and then nodded and said quietly, "I think that's a real good idea. I don't think I could ever get these corrals finished on time without some help."

Avery nodded, surprised at how much talking he'd done. "Thanks," he said.

∽ ∽

The two men entered the hotel, and glancing through the restaurant door, Avery saw that the boy's mother was waiting tables. She was wearing the same gray dress.

"You go on in," he told Wally. "I'll just take a room and then I'll join you."

Wally nodded and entered the restaurant. Avery rang the bell and waited. Again, he heard the quick footsteps and turned to see a startled look on Mrs. Harper's face. Before she had a chance to say anything, Avery spoke. "Don't worry, ma'am. I'll take care not to run you over this time."

She smiled uncertainly and said, "It was just as much my fault. I wasn't watching where I was going."

There was an awkward pause and then Avery said, "I guess I'll be needin' a room for a few days."

"Do you plan to stay in it this time?"

"Yes, ma'am. I hope that wasn't a bother."

"Not at all. I don't know why I brought it up."

Avery signed for his room, got his key, and then cleared his throat. "Excuse me, ma'am," he said. "I was just wonderin' …"

Mrs. Harper waited expectantly while Avery fidgeted with his room key. Their eyes met briefly and then Avery looked quickly down at the register and then back to her, but she offered no encouragement.

"I was just wonderin'," he continued, shifting his weight nervously, "well you see, ma'am, I'm gonna need to hire someone to help peel some rails. I'll be workin' with Mr. Gibbs for a few days 'cause he needs to get them corrals built before the snow flies." Avery glanced at Mrs. Harper, who was watching him with a puzzled expression, and then, looking away, he continued. "He tells me you have a fine boy who's a good, hard worker, you see, and I was just wonderin' if you'd let him work with me and Wally for about three afternoons. I know he's a kid an' all, so we wouldn't work him too hard." Avery couldn't believe how nervous he felt, and he'd been staring at the hotel register the whole time he'd been speaking.

Now he raised his eyes again to meet the girl's, and he couldn't read what hers were saying. "'Course if you don't like the idea, ma'am …"

"Oh no," she said quickly. "I think Peter would like to work for you and Mr. Gibbs. It's just that …" Mrs. Harper bit her bottom lip, looked down at the floor, then back to Avery. "He's only just turned six," she said. "Are you sure he could do it?"

Avery felt a huge sense of relief. "Any boy his age can use a pocketknife. It ain't hard work, ma'am. I'll just be too busy draggin' rails to do much peelin'. Wally'll be around to keep an eye on the little fella."

"Mr. Gibbs is a kind man," Mrs. Harper said.

"I reckon he is at that," Avery agreed.

"When would you want Peter to be there?"

"Would tomorrow just after lunch be okay?" Avery asked. "I'll need some time in the mornin' to get him some rails skidded down."

"I'm sure that would be fine. I think he'll be quite excited."

Avery was glad that Mrs. Harper seemed pleased. For a moment there was silence, and then, glancing toward the restaurant door, she said, "I'd best get back to waiting tables."

Another thought had been working at the back of Avery's mind, but he was unsure and thought maybe he'd best leave well enough alone. He was gaining confidence, however, so as Mrs. Harper turned to leave, he blurted out, "Um, there's just one other thing if you don't mind?"

She turned back to face him, a question on her brow. "What is it?" she asked.

Avery drew a deep breath, shifted his weight from one foot to the other, then said, "Well, ma'am, I seen you

56

had some dress goods in the store the other day when I run into you, and I was wonderin' if you might do some sewin'?"

"I do a little seamstress work on the side, yes," Mrs. Harper said, her eyes still questioning but curious.

"Well that's real good 'cause I need a dress sewed for a special lady, and I'd like for you to make it."

"Who is this special lady?" Mrs. Harper asked.

Avery pretended not to hear her question and continued speaking. "I want it to be a real pretty dress," he said, "and this girl's about exactly your size, so if you make it to fit you, it'll be about right."

"Are you sure?"

"Yes, ma'am. I'm sure, real sure," Avery said. "I don't know too much about dresses though, so you just make it how you think it would be real pretty, 'cause I really want this girl to like it."

"All right, I'll do it," Mrs. Harper said.

"Thanks," Avery said with feeling. "I'll just have some supper and then head across to the mercantile and pick up the fabric. Then I'll come back here and give it to you."

A look of concern washed across Mrs. Harper's face, and she said, "I'm off work in half an hour. Peter spends the afternoons at the Conklin's, and Mrs. Conklin will be dropping him off at home shortly, so I need to be there."

"I could bring it by your house. That way I could talk with your son and explain things to him."

Mrs. Harper hesitated a moment and then somewhat reluctantly agreed. "That will be fine I suppose."

"Is there a problem?" Avery asked.

"No, not really." Then in a voice that betrayed frustration, she said, "Mrs. Parker who lives next door will make it her business to tell the town that I've had a strange man come calling; that's all."

"Not to worry, ma'am. I can stay outside on the street the whole time where she can see me. Would that work for you?"

"That will be fine. She'll talk anyway, no matter what. Thank you Mr. ...?"

"Carson, Avery Carson. Recently of Texas."

Then in a frank and friendly manner, the pretty girl in the gray dress said, "My name's Emily Harper."

Avery was startled at the name, remembering the Emily who'd signed the Bible. It showed in his eyes, and Mrs. Harper, seeing it, cautiously asked, "Is something wrong?"

"No, no," Avery said quickly, "I was just surprised at your name. I was thinkin' of another Emily."

"Is Emily the special lady I'm sewing the dress for?"

Avery's face broke into a smile. "Yes, ma'am, she is as a matter of fact," he said.

Mrs. Harper smiled a wistful smile, and for a moment, her thoughts seemed far away. Then she said, "Our house is the last one on the west end of town, right next to the river. I'll tell Peter you're coming."

Avery waited a few moments before following her into the restaurant, and his heart was beating rapidly. Wally was seated at the same table Avery had used on his last visit, and he'd left him the seat with its back to the wall.

Avery sat down across from him and said, "Well, Mr. Gibbs, I just hired you a rail peeler."

"Good, good," Wally said. "When does he start?"

"Tomorrow afternoon."

Wally laughed. "I guess that means you're gonna have to get busy cuttin' and skiddin' rails," he said.

"I was figurin' on it," Avery replied.

Mrs. Harper came over to their table, filled their coffee cups, and took their orders. Nothing was said about Peter and the fact that he'd be working with them the following day, but Avery sensed that she was pleased and wanted to be friendly without seeming too familiar.

While they were waiting for their meals to be served, Avery said, "I've had quite the adventure since the last time I was in town."

"Oh," Wally said, sounding curious. "Tell me about it."

Avery began to tell him everything that had happened, his story interrupted briefly when Mrs. Harper brought their food. Both men thanked her, and then Avery continued while they ate.

Wally Gibbs was completely taken by the tale, and other than a couple of comments and questions, was silent throughout.

"So, Wally," Avery said, "I'm figurin' you musta met this fella, and I'm wonderin' what you can tell me about him."

Wally shook his head. "That's what's kinda queer. I'm sure he was never around here. If he had of been, I would've known. It's not a big town, and anyone comin' through has to stop at the barn."

Avery looked surprised. "How can that be? He had to pack in from somewhere, and he'd need to get supplies from time to time."

Wally shrugged. "I don't know," he said. "He musta followed that valley in from the south or the north. He maybe didn't even know we had a town out here. Bow City's only seven years old. Maybe he was here before that."

"Are there any settlements north or south of here?" Avery asked.

"There's been a fair bit of minin' in the mountains north of here a ways. Maybe he drifted down from Montana. Could be there's a pass over the mountains south of here to some settlements. I don't know. What I do know, though, is that he never came through here— not as long as I've lived here anyways. And that's goin' on five years."

Both men ate in silence for a while. Both were deep in thought. Then Wally said, "I wonder what Albert Ball at the Double Diamond would say if he knew someone was livin' up west of the gap. Near as I can figure, he's thinkin' once his herd's built up, that grass up there will be his."

Avery looked up from his food and said thoughtfully, "I suppose that makes a kind of sense. It'd be good summer pasture for sure. Anyway, I'm figurin' on stayin' for the winter. After that, I don't know. If I like it and none of this fella's relatives have a prior claim, I just might stake it out myself."

"Did you see any cattle sign up there? How was this gent makin' a living?"

"Nope. I never saw no sign of cattle. I didn't really take the time to scout around though. If the weather holds, I'd like to ride south and see if I can pick up a trail to someplace. I rode pretty far north, and the valley sorta petered out. I'm guessin' he packed his things in from the south. After we eat, I'll head over and have a talk with the sheriff. What did you say his name was?"

"Coleman. Ernie Coleman."

"Anyway, I figure if I'm set on stayin' around for a while, I best go make some peace talk. He may be able to track down some information on the CP brand that buckskin's packin' too."

After supper, Wally Gibbs headed back to the barn while Avery stood for a moment on the boardwalk outside the hotel. Although he knew it was something he needed to do, he was reluctant to go see the sheriff after their last meeting. He'd been feeling unusually relaxed and talkative over the past hour, but now a familiar reserve settled on him like an unwelcome cloud. Seeing the saddle shop next to the sheriff's office, he remembered he'd need a new cinch before he started dragging rails, so he decided to head there first. He'd see about a new packsaddle while he was at it.

He paused before stepping onto the street to let a buggy pass on its way to the barn. It was pulled by two smart-looking bays, and Avery noticed the Double Diamond on the right shoulder of the nearest horse. The driver was a big, barrel-chested man with an iron gray moustache. His passenger was a petite young lady with a full head of rich, auburn hair that spilled out from under a dark blue travel bonnet that matched the dress she wore. Their eyes met, and Avery instinctively nodded and touched the brim of his hat. The driver, looking straight ahead, never saw him.

A few minutes later, Avery emerged from the saddle shop with a sawbuck and lash cinch over his shoulder, as well as a cinch for his saddle. He realized then that he'd have to drop off his things at the barn before visiting the sheriff, and he decided he'd best go pick up the dress material and take it to Mrs. Harper first and then go see the sheriff.

He turned for the barn and noticed the man and the girl from the buggy were just entering the hotel. For some reason, he was relieved that they wouldn't be at the barn when he got there. He heard Wally hammering out back but hung his packsaddle on a rail and left without speaking to him.

CHAPTER SEVEN

McFadden and a fat woman were stocking shelves when Avery entered the mercantile. He ignored them and, feeling self-conscious, headed straight for the rear aisle and the dress goods. He found the silky green cloth Mrs. Harper had been admiring, but realized he had no idea how much to buy. Reluctantly, he put the whole bolt of cloth under his arm and headed for the front counter. He hoped McFadden wouldn't ask too many questions, but it was the fat woman who came to wait on him. She had curly, strawberry blonde hair piled in a careless bun on top of her head, and her flabby cheeks were red from exertion.

"That fancy cloth is for makin' a dress out of," she told him.

"Yes, ma'am. It's for a lady."

"Well I didn't figure it'd be for you!" she said and then threw back her head and laughed. The laugh ended abruptly, and her bright green eyes snapped to his. "Who's the lady?" she asked.

"Someone who needs a dress," Avery drawled, looking down at the counter and shifting his weight from one foot to another.

The woman laughed again, and Avery found it irritating. "Well, we wouldn't want no lady runnin' around in her petticoats, now would we?" she said, smiling as she leaned her heavy forearms on the counter.

Avery was unsure how to proceed, and for a moment he stood awkwardly, aware that no sound was coming from the aisle where McFadden was working. Finally he mumbled, "I ain't sure how much cloth to buy."

"How big is this woman? Is she from around here? I know everybody hereabouts."

"She's about average size I reckon."

"Who is she? If you tell me who she is, I could tell you exactly how much cloth you'll need."

"I'm from down Texas way, ma'am. Do you know all the ladies in Texas?"

This time the laugh made Avery wince. "Well, let's just say this lady's about my size," the fat woman said. "You figure that'd do?"

"Yes, ma'am, that'd be enough I reckon."

"I'll just measure you out five yards then. That way I'll be sure."

Avery thanked her, paid for the cloth, and asked for a sack to carry it in. He was relieved that McFadden had his back to him as he left and seemed to pay him no mind.

Instead of heading down the main street, Avery crossed to the hotel, took a well-worn path between two buildings, and followed the alley west. He was still reluctant to meet people, and he didn't want to walk past the sheriff's office just yet. He reached the end of the alley, turned toward the river, and saw the Harper house huddled low and small, not quite part of the town, not quite off by itself. Behind a rail fence, a few stubborn, brown leaves clung to the lilac bushes on each side of a sagging weathered gate. Avery paused, remembering his promise to stay in view out on the street, but not wanting to appear standoffish. It seemed condescending and rude to stand there and holler, so after a brief moment of indecision, he opened the gate. As he did so, the front door of the house swung open, and Emily Harper stepped outside.

"Hello, Mr. Carson," she said.

"Howdy, ma'am," Avery replied, touching his hat brim. "Here's the material for the dress." He stood rooted in his tracks as she came forward to take the sack from him. As she examined the cloth, Peter came to stand shyly at his mother's side.

"This is beautiful material, Mr. Carson," Emily said. "Do you know what style of dress you want me to make?"

"No, ma'am."

Emily looked up from the material to Avery, and as their eyes met, he continued awkwardly. "Like I said before, I don't know too much about dresses. Could you just make it how you think it'd be pretty?"

She smiled and nodded. "I'll do my best to make a beautiful dress for your Emily, Mr. Carson."

"Thank you, ma'am."

Placing a hand on Peter's shoulder, Emily said, "Peter, this is Mr. Carson, the man I told you about."

Avery turned to the boy, who was watching him with big eyes; held out his right hand; and said, "Howdy, Peter. Did your ma tell you what I'd like for you to do?"

Peter shook his hand and said, "Yes, sir, Mr. Carson."

"Would you be willin' to give me a hand then? I'd pay you of course."

Peter looked at Avery with a serious expression, nodded, and said, "Yes, sir. I'd like to do it, only I've never peeled any rails before."

"It ain't hard," Avery replied. "It just takes time, and we might not have a lotta time before winter sets in. I'll likely be able to do some of the peelin' myself, but I gotta cut and skid them rails down from the hills first. You got a good knife, son?"

"No, sir."

Avery pretended concern and to think a moment before he spoke. Then he said, "Mostly a fella wants to peel rails with a drawknife. I figure that might be a bit awkward for you to handle though. I'll likely be needin' my knife, so it won't do for me to lend you mine." Avery paused for a moment with his hand on his chin.

Emily was watching Peter, who was staring intently at Avery with a worried expression.

"Tell you what," Avery said. "If you don't mind spendin' some of the money you'll be makin' on a new pocketknife, I could pay you somethin' in advance. You could head over to the mercantile and buy yourself one. Would that work for you?"

Peter looked at him wide-eyed. "You mean the knife would be mine?" he asked unbelievingly.

"'Course it would be yours. I don't need another one. Here," Avery said, digging some coins from his pocket, "this should do you. Only make sure you buy a good one. I want you to buy the best one they got so it won't break when you're peelin' them rails. Understand?"

"Yes, sir," Peter said eagerly as he took the money. He then looked up at his mother as if to ask if it was okay.

She smiled warmly at him and said, "Go put it in the drawer by your bed, Peter. We'll go buy a knife in the morning."

Peter looked back at Avery and said, "Thanks for the job, Mr. Carson. I think I'll be real good at peeling rails." He then turned and ran through the open door of the house.

Avery and Mrs. Harper watched him go, and then Avery touched his hat and said, "Be seein' you, ma'am."

As he turned to leave, Mrs. Harper said, "Mr. Carson?"

He turned back to face her.

"Thank you," she said. "I think maybe the reason we ran into each other in the store was because we were both looking at the same thing."

Avery looked down at his feet embarrassed and nodded, "I didn't like the way that fella talked to your boy, that's all. Strikes me he's a fine boy."

Avery looked up, and their eyes met. He turned then

and left, and neither of them spoke. Emily watched him as he walked away and then turned and entered the house, closing the door behind her.

Avery drew a deep breath and let it out. That had been tough, real tough. It had seemed like a good enough plan when he'd dreamed it up out there in the big, wide open. Pulling it off had been another thing altogether. He had to admit though that he felt good, better than he'd felt in ages.

Some movement caught his attention, and he looked up to see the girl from the buggy walking straight toward him. She glanced at him and then over at the Harper house, and he realized that, from the direction he was walking, he could have only been one place. There was no need for an explanation, but remembering the town gossip, he reluctantly drew up as the young lady approached. She was a pretty girl, with a clean, fresh face and deep green eyes. Because Avery had stopped, she did too, studying him in a curious but friendly manner. Avery felt that, because he had stopped first, he needed to speak first, but he had no idea what to say.

Finally he said, "Howdy, ma'am. I seen you in the buggy earlier."

"And I saw you in front of the hotel. We don't get many visitors out this way so I was curious. Is this your first time in Bow City?"

"No, ma'am. I was here about a week ago."

A knowing light came into the girl's eyes. "Ah," she said. "You wouldn't be the desperate character that Sheriff Coleman ran out of town the other day?" She said it with a hint of mischief in her voice, and if she thought he was a desperate character, she gave no indication.

"That could be me all right," Avery responded apologetically.

"Well, I'd say he didn't do a very good job of it."

"No, ma'am. I guess not." Avery shifted his weight from one foot to the other and then gestured with his thumb toward Emily Harper's house and said, "I'm hirin' young Peter to peel some rails."

"Are you an acquaintance of the Harpers?" the girl asked.

"No, ma'am. Wally Gibbs over at the barn mentioned them to me. I'm helpin' him build some new corrals."

The girl seemed satisfied with the explanation. She smiled and said, "I'm heading to Emily's myself. She's sewing me a new dress for the Thanksgiving Dance." She then extended her hand and said, "My name's Carol Ball. My daddy owns the Double Diamond, a ranch west of town. If you're staying around these parts, stop in. We're hosting the dance."

"Thanks, ma'am," Avery said. "I'm Avery Carson, recently of Texas. I ain't too much for dancin', but we'll see."

Carol waved good-bye, and Avery touched his hat brim and then headed for the main street. Again he drew in a deep breath and let it out, shaking his head.

No one was in the sheriff's office, so Avery helped himself

to a chair by the front wall and settled down to wait. The office was in a small, bare room, and its furnishings consisted of the chair he was in, a scuffed and scarred desk with a leather padded swivel chair, and a potbellied stove. Behind the desk was a gun rack that held one rifle and a double-barrel shotgun. Avery guessed it was the same gun the sheriff had used the day they'd had their confrontation in the saloon. On the back wall was an open door leading to a small cell block.

He didn't have long to wait before he heard boots on the boardwalk and a happy-go-lucky whistle. The door opened, and Sheriff Ernie Coleman stepped in, walking straight to his desk where he deposited a stack of mail.

"Howdy, Sheriff," Avery drawled.

Coleman spun around to face him, the startled look on his face quickly giving way to one of anger as recognition came to him. "You again," he said. "I thought I told you to leave town."

Avery had his first good look at the sheriff and, without getting to his feet, studied him a moment before speaking. Coleman was a slim man of medium height in his late twenties or early thirties. Save for the silver star pinned to his shirt pocket, he was dressed like any rider. He had a good-looking, clean-shaven face, marred by a nose that had been broken and set badly. Avery noticed too that he was left-handed, with his pistol holstered for a cross draw on the right-hand side. Avery uncrossed his legs and leaned forward, his elbows on his knees. "I did leave town," he said. "You never told me I couldn't come back."

"Don't get smart with me, cowboy. We don't want your type in Bow City."

"Just what is my type, Sheriff Coleman?" Avery asked.

A flicker of surprise touched Coleman's eyes at Avery's use of his name and then was gone. "A gun slick saddle tramp, too lazy to hold a job and thinking he's smarter and tougher than anyone who does."

Avery got slowly to his feet and said, "The name's Avery Carson, recently of Texas. What we was doin' in the saloon is called gamblin'. The reason it's called gamblin' is 'cause sometimes you win and sometimes you lose. I had a lucky streak goin', and them gents didn't like it. They was fixin' to use their six-shooters to take the gamble out of the gamblin'. I got the drop on 'em, and that's when you came in. Now I don't need to tell you none of this Sheriff Ernie Coleman, but I'm tellin' you 'cause I aim to be a good citizen. I'm gonna be around town for a few days 'cause I'm *workin'* for Wally over at the barn. If you still want to run me out of town, you best bring some help. Anyway, you'd do your job a sight better if you wasn't so quick to jump to conclusions."

Coleman's eyes smoldered. "Don't tell me how to do my job, mister!" he snapped.

"I just did. Good day, Ernie."

Avery dismissed him and walked out the door. It wasn't until he was halfway to the barn that he remembered he hadn't asked about the CP brand on his buckskin.

CHAPTER EIGHT

Avery was up early the next morning. The restaurant wasn't open, so he crossed the street to the barn and saddled his horse. He pulled his rifle from its scabbard and replaced it with an ax. Wally had left him a short piece of chain to wrap around the rails so he wouldn't damage his catch rope with the dragging. With everything ready, he headed back to the hotel.

The restaurant door was open, and he took his usual seat against the back wall. A short, middle-aged woman took his order and then disappeared through the kitchen door. Avery guessed she was chief cook and bottle washer this morning, as they wouldn't bother hiring a waitress at this early hour.

He was about halfway through a breakfast of bacon and flapjacks, when Coleman entered the room. The sheriff stopped short when he saw Avery, his jaw tensing and his eyes growing hard.

Avery realized he was going to have to do a better job of making peace with the sheriff if he intended to stick around. He knew he had nothing against him really and that the circumstances had just gotten them off to a bad start. He decided now was as good a time as any.

"Mornin', Sheriff," he said. "Why don't you have a seat?"

Avery could tell Coleman wasn't at all crazy about the idea but had little option but to accept the invitation. He sat down opposite Avery, his back stiff, wanting to appear in charge, but his face betraying his uncertainty.

Avery felt uncomfortable himself, but after a moment, he set his fork down and wiped his mouth with the back of his hand. "I was meanin' to ask you, Sheriff Coleman," he said, "if you knew who owned the CP brand. I found a horse back through the gap west of here that's packin' it on his left hip."

Coleman studied Avery for a moment, on his guard but curious. "No one in these parts uses that brand. This horse was just running loose out there?"

The short lady came and filled Avery's coffee and took the sheriff's order. When she'd left for the kitchen, Avery explained about finding the buildings and the dead man and what he'd done. He told nothing of his fight with the Indians. When he was finished, he downed the last of his coffee, and looked at the sheriff.

"I had no idea anyone was living out that way," Coleman said. "I wonder who he was and where he came from?"

Avery got to his feet as the waitress brought the sheriff's food to the table. "That's what I'm wonderin' too," he said.

"That's why I'd like you to look into who owns that brand. Maybe we can track down the man's next of kin."

"I'll see what I can do."

Avery nodded his thanks and headed for the door. He had to step aside as Carol Ball and the big man he assumed was her father entered the restaurant. She gave him a smile and a little wave, while the man with the iron gray moustache paid him no mind at all. While he was paying for his meal, he saw that Sheriff Coleman was carrying his plate over to join them at their table.

✎ ✎

The work proved slower going than he had anticipated, but by noon, Avery managed to have twelve rails cut and skidded down to the corral. Wally Gibbs, who was working on tamping a corner post, set his bar aside and walked over to where Avery was tying his horse.

"I packed us some lunch," he said. "Didn't think it was right you should be buyin' your meals when you're workin' for free."

Avery thanked him.

"No, thank you," Wally said. "I can't tell you how much I appreciate the help."

Both men sat down, their faces to the sun and their backs against the corral rails. They ate in silence, enjoying the rest, the food, and the easy company. They were just finishing up when Mrs. Harper and young Peter walked through the double doors at the back of the barn.

Avery was the first to his feet, and he met them half

way across the corral. "Afternoon, Mrs. Harper, Peter," he said, acknowledging the boy with a nod.

Mrs. Harper smiled, "Good afternoon, Mr. Carson. Hello, Mr. Gibbs."

Wally Gibbs stopped beside Avery and said, "Afternoon, ma'am."

"I bought a knife, Mr. Carson," Peter said, excitement showing in his eyes.

"Did you now," Avery said. "Mind if I see it. I want to make sure you bought a good one."

Emily smiled down at her son as he dug deep into his pocket. He proudly produced the pretty, red-handled knife with the ivory inlay on the handle.

Avery let out a whistle as he took the knife. "Now that's a fine knife, son," he said. "That should work real good for peelin' rails. It might get a little sticky from the pitch, but don't you worry, we'll clean it up good when we're done." Handing the knife back to Peter he said, "Just step on over here for a minute, and I'll show you what you'll be doin'."

Peter and his mother followed Avery over to the stack of freshly cut rails, and Wally went back to his tamping. Avery stooped and grabbed the big end of a rail, dragged it over and propped it up on the corral so it was out of the dirt.

"Now look here," he said. "Some of the bark's already come off from the draggin', so I don't think it'll be too tough. Can I see your knife again?"

Peter handed him the knife and watched intently as

Avery opened it and demonstrated how he should go about the peeling.

"Now with this type of knife, you should always cut away from yourself. I'm sure you know all this stuff already, so don't mind my blabbin'. Anyway, if you're cuttin' away from yourself like this, and you do happen to slip, you won't get cut, understand?"

"Yes, Mr. Carson."

"When you get done peelin' one side, just get me or Mr. Gibbs there to help flip the rail over. When you finish a rail, we'll help set you up with another one. Figure you can handle that?"

"I think so, Mr. Carson. I can see why I needed to buy a good knife."

Avery chuckled. "Well get to it then, Peter. And don't be afraid to take a break if you get tired. It's a big job you're tacklin'."

"Yes, sir."

"I'll see you later, Peter," Mrs. Harper said. "I'll stop by and pick you up after work."

Avery walked with her as far as the back of the barn. It surprised him when she stopped and her eyes lingered on his horse. "Mr. Carson, is that your horse?" she asked.

"Yes, ma'am."

She turned to him, her face serious. "We've never met before, have we?"

Avery was startled by her question. "No, ma'am," he said. What he was thinking and didn't say was that, if he'd ever met her before, he couldn't possibly have forgotten.

She turned and looked at the horse again and then back to him. "Have you ever been to Denver?" she asked.

"No, ma'am. I've been up the trail to Kansas three times, but that's about it."

"You remind me of someone," Emily said. "I didn't notice it at first, but now I can't help it. He had the same accent and a horse just like yours. Strange." She turned and left, walking up the alley through the barn. Avery stood and watched her go.

"Strange," he echoed. He shook his head and then went to his horse and mounted up.

❧   ❧

They finished the corrals in two days. Peter developed a blister on his knife hand after the first day, so Avery bought him the smallest leather gloves he could find. They were too big, but Peter was pleased with them.

When the last rail was spiked in place, Wally said, "Well thanks, men. I figure we make a first-class crew. I also figure I owe you both supper over at the restaurant."

"Well that sounds fine by me," Avery said. "What do you figure there, young fella?"

"I ain't never ate at the restaurant before," Peter said. "Ma says it's real expensive."

"For poor folks like you an' me it is," Avery agreed. "However, for a rich fella like Mr. Gibbs here, it ain't nothin'."

"I'd like to eat in the restaurant," Peter said. "Only ma

would skin me alive if I went in there without cleaning up first."

Avery and Wally laughed.

"I need to clean up some too," Avery said. "How's about we head over to the hotel. I got a washbasin in my room, so we can both get respectable. Then we'll meet Mr. Gibbs after he's gone home and washed off. Look at him. He's dirtier than the both of us put together."

"Sure," Peter said eagerly. "I've never been in the hotel either."

⚬⚬   ⚬⚬

Up in his hotel room, Avery poured a basin of water for Peter. It was cold but, for the most part, did the job. When Peter was through, Avery dumped the dirty water out the window and refilled the basin. He stripped off his shirt and began washing up while Peter sat on the bed.

"How did you get that scar on your side, Mr. Carson?" Peter asked.

"A Comanche knife," Avery said.

"What happened to the Comanche?"

Avery didn't answer right away and then he said, "I don't think your ma would like it if we talk too much about fightin'."

"She wouldn't mind. She says that, most times, fighting's not good, but sometimes, you need to. Have you done a lot of fighting Mr. Carson?"

"You ever hear of the Texas Rangers?" Avery asked.

"No, sir."

"Well, bein' in the Rangers is kinda' like bein' a sheriff. Yeah, I've done some fightin'—more than I cared to I'm afraid. Let's not talk about it to your ma though. I don't like talkin' about fightin' when there's a lady present."

"Ma has a pistol hid under her apron behind the front door. Her ma and pa were killed in the Sioux Uprising in Minnesota. Sometimes ma's scarred 'cause our house is on the edge of town. That's why she has the pistol. That and for any vermin that might come along. I don't know what a vermin is. Do you, Mr. Carson?"

Avery was buttoning up a clean shirt. "Just so as your ma knows," he said. "I guess that's all that really matters. Let's go eat."

Peter slid off the bed. "Are you gonna marry that girl that ma's makin' the dress for?" he asked.

"Now where did you hear I had a girl?" Avery asked.

"Ma told Miss Ball when she came to pick up her dress. Miss Ball said you were a handsome man and that she hoped you'd come to the Thanksgiving Dance. Ma told her she was out of luck 'cause you already had a girl and that you were having her make a dress for her."

Avery felt his ears getting red. "Do you always talk this much?" he asked.

"Only with my friends," Peter said.

Avery smiled. "I reckon I'm kinda that way myself. I hope I ain't been talkin' your ear off."

Peter looked at him seriously, shook his head, and said, "Nope."

"Well let's go eat then. I'm near about starved. Oh, wait a minute; I almost forgot to pay you." Avery dug in his pocket and counted out one dollar in coins. "Here you go. And thanks for all your hard work."

Peter looked at the coins wide-eyed. "Thanks, Mr. Carson. I really liked working for you."

⧢ ⧢

Wally was in the restaurant when they got there, and once again, he'd left the seat against the back wall for Avery. Peter slid in first, and Avery sat down beside him.

Mrs. Harper came into the room and looked questioningly at them.

"We got done ahead of time, Mrs. Harper," Wally said. "I figure it's on account of the fact that I had such a good crew. We're celebratin', and supper's on me."

"Well," Mrs. Harper said smiling, "this will be quite a treat for Peter. It's only fair to warn you though; he's got a big appetite."

"Not to worry. Oh and, Mrs. Harper, I ain't talked this over with Mr. Carson and Peter yet, but if it's okay with you, and seein' how we got done ahead of schedule, I figured tomorrow would be a good day for the three of us men to go fishin'."

Emily looked at Wally, and her eyes betrayed her appreciation. She then looked at Peter, who was watching her hopefully. "Thank you, Mr. Gibbs," she said. "That sounds like a great idea. Only please keep a close eye on Peter. He doesn't know how to swim."

"Will do, ma'am," Wally said.

Avery looked at Mrs. Harper and nodded that he was in agreement.

CHAPTER NINE

Two days later, his packhorse loaded with supplies, Avery mounted up ready to head for the gap. On an impulse, he pulled up in front of the sheriff's office, dismounted, and tied his horses at the hitching rail.

Sheriff Coleman looked up from his desk as Avery entered. "No one in this territory's registered a CP brand," he said before Avery had a chance to speak.

Avery took the chair by the wall and sat for a moment, deep in thought. He was remembering Mrs. Harper's unusual comments at the corral, a ghost of an idea nibbling at his brain. "I'm wonderin' if it ain't a Texas brand," he said. Looking up quickly, he asked. "Would you have a pen and paper I could use? I think I need to write a letter."

"Sure," Coleman said in a businesslike tone. Then, after a brief hesitation, he added, "I was about to step out, so I suppose you could use my desk."

"Thanks. And thanks for lookin' into this so quick."

"Not a problem. Albert Ball at the Double Diamond is also interested in finding out who's been living out there."

Avery remembered Wally's comments about Ball wanting to use the grass in the gap, and he decided he'd best write a second letter. If the man he'd buried had filed on his place, a record at the land office would tell him who he was. If Clancy hadn't filed on it, then Avery decided he would. That way, he could establish a legal claim in case problems arose in the future.

The first letter he wrote was to Willy Paulson back in Texas. Avery had intended to just write a quick note and ask him to check into the CP brand, but it ended up being a long letter.

It was an enjoyable ride back to the gap, and Avery took it at a leisurely pace. He smiled as he passed Wally's fishing hole, remembering Peter's excitement when he'd managed to land a good-sized trout. The gelding picked up his pace of his own accord as they neared the gap, and Avery felt a growing sense of anticipation. The roar from the river grew steadily louder as the grade grew steeper and the channel narrowed. He looked ahead at the two overlapping gray ridges of stone and marveled again at how well hidden the pass was. Just before riding through the notch, he stopped to let his horses blow and watched the wild, tumbling water foam and crash down the stone-walled canyon below him.

"This'd be a scary place when the river's in flood," he told his horse, who cocked an ear toward him. It was a mesmerizing scene, but he pulled his gaze away and moved off at an easy trot.

Avery had a lot of things he wanted to do, and he hoped the good weather would hold. First thing in the morning, he'd move his supplies from his gap campsite back to the cabin. Then he wanted to follow the creek up behind the buildings and see if a hanging valley actually was hidden up there. After that, he hoped he'd have time to ride south and maybe figure out where Clancy had packed in from.

The sun had dropped behind the mountains when Avery rode into the yard. It felt good to be back, and he wondered why this should be. He'd only spent a short time at the place, but it felt like home. He tied off in front of the cabin, unpacked his supplies, and then headed for the barn to off saddle. After turning out the horses, he carried the food down to the root cellar. By then it was almost dark, and he lit the lamps, built a fire in the woodstove, and cooked his supper. All was quiet and peaceful, and he was content.

Later that night when he'd cleaned up his dishes, he took the Bible, sat down at the table, and pulled a lamp close. The Bible fell open at a place with a large underlined portion, so he read it. It was a description of what love should be—patient and kind, keeping no record of wrong, always believing, always hoping, and always enduring. He read it and then reread it and then read it a third time. The words were like music that touched the depths of his soul.

He closed the Bible and sat back, his head against the wall. He was remembering Audrey, and for the first time, he allowed himself to frame a question that he knew had been crouching at the edge of his consciousness for a long time. He wondered if Audrey had ever loved him. He knew she was in love with what she thought he'd become and he had done his best not to disappoint her. Another thought came to him that he'd never considered before, and then he knew he wasn't being entirely fair to Audrey. Had he ever really loved her?

He'd looked up to her father because he was the biggest rancher in the territory, and he'd been flattered when Audrey had chosen him over all the other young men in the area and her father had approved. It hit him then that she'd chosen him because he was the best up-and-comer and he'd chosen her because he wanted to be what she believed he could be. If their love had been less than it should have been, they were both equally to blame. He wondered, though, if anyone could love the way he'd just read about. He looked over at the Bible. When he opened it up again, these words seemed to jump off the page. "For God so loved the world that he gave his only begotten Son, that whosoever believeth in him should not perish but have everlasting life."

Avery closed the book again and sat quietly while a warm wind whispered beneath the eaves. After a time, he got to his feet and blew out the lamp. That night, he slept in the bed.

~~~ ~~~

Avery was back home with his supplies by midmorning. The air was crisp and still after a hard frost, but an ambitious sun was climbing the blue sky, doing its best to hold off winter. Avery fixed a quick lunch, and by the time he was riding up the canyon behind the house, he had to shed his jacket, and the frost on the grass had turned to sparkling drops of water.

His packhorse followed as far as the gate at the top of the horse pasture, and from there, the grade grew steep and the buckskin had to lower his head and dig in. The trail was well worn, and it wound its way between shrubs and boulders, roughly following the tumbling creek, before beginning to level off. Ahead, the canyon sides grew lower but became steep and narrow like a gun sight, and Avery could see a rail fence blocking his way. He rode up to a gate, and the first thing he noticed was old cattle sign on the other side. About seventy-five yards ahead was another rail fence and gate, and beyond that, the canyon appeared to open up, and he could see some grass and a cow and calf grazing.

His curiosity aroused, he dismounted, opened the gate, and led his horse through. He was now in a sort of holding yard formed by the canyon walls on two sides and the rail fences on either end, with the creek flowing roughly down the middle. Where he was standing, the corral was only about forty feet across, but it looked to be at least twice that at the far end. He led his horse to the next gate, where he stopped short in disbelief and amazement. He was looking at a beautiful, grassy basin, roughly four hundred acres in size, hemmed in on three sides by snow-covered peaks. Scattered across the valley floor, knee deep in grass, were about eighty head of cattle. They looked to be a mix of cows, calves, yearlings, and two-year-olds, and the closest ones to him had their heads up, eyeing him warily. As far as he could see, the younger stuff was all white-faced or brockle-faced, and the older cows were your typical longhorns.

Once through the gate, Avery mounted up and began a wide, slow circle around the valley. He came upon one, and then two white-faced bulls, and he was impressed by the good hip and beefy hindquarters of their offspring. The cattle were branded CP on the left hip, but none of this year's calves had been castrated or branded. As he rode, many questions came to mind. Did these cows winter up here? He'd seen no cattle sign down below, and there was no hay put up. Maybe every other summer, Clancy had put up hay, but this year, his death had come before he'd had a chance to get started. Where had he sold his beef? Avery wondered. Were the two-year-olds his first calf crop? Maybe the cattle had managed to winter up here, but now with the increase in herd size, shortage of grass could become a problem. He drew up on a sun-soaked side hill and dismounted.

With his reins trailing, Avery sat down on a flat rock to consider his options. His ride south would have to be put off. He was going to wean the calves, castrate and brand them, give them time to heal up, and then drive them along with the two-year-old steers back through the gap and see if he could sell them. It might be hard trying to get rid of the calves, but with a small herd like this one, too much inbreeding could be a problem. He'd try the Double Diamond first, as it was the closest.

He wondered about the legality of selling someone else's cattle and decided that, if he discovered some relative had a claim to them, he'd turn the money and the place over while keeping thirty dollars a month as wages for himself. He lingered a while longer, enjoying the afternoon sun and then mounted up, finished his circle, and headed back down the canyon.

The following evening, Avery went to bed early, serenaded by the distant sound of bawling cattle. He'd pushed the herd into the holding area and cut everything except the calves and two-year-old steers back. Then he'd put the steers through the lower gate and branded the calves, castrating all but two of the better bull calves. His hope was that the promise of some white-faced breeding stock would make it easier to negotiate a sale. When he'd finished, he'd moved the calves in with the steers and hoped the two fences would keep them and their mothers apart. He was beat, and sleep was not long in coming.

The next four days were spent close to home. Avery had found a couple of broadaxes in the storage shed and decided he'd like to learn to use them. He skidded in two pine logs, sawed them into twelve-foot lengths, and then spent most of an afternoon trying to make a square timber. His first attempt was a complete failure, and he ended up sawing the log up for firewood. He was definitely gaining a new appreciation for what it had taken to build the cabin and outbuildings. The next day, he was hard at it again, and this time, though he was painstakingly slow, the results were better. By the end of the third day, he had four timbers that were usable.

It was almost dark when he finished up. His shoulders were sore, his arms were weary, and he was too tired to bother with cooking. He ate a can of cold beans by lamplight and then read another underlined section from the Bible. It was a story about some angry men, religious leaders, who brought a woman to Jesus who had been caught in the act of adultery. They wanted to kill her because that's what the law said they were entitled to do. Even more though, they wanted to get Jesus in trouble with the law, so they asked him what they should do. Here Avery came to the end of the page. Instead of turning it immediately, he sat for a while, trying to guess what Jesus's answer would be. He had no idea, so with anticipation, he turned the page.

"He that is without sin among you, let him first cast a stone at her."

Avery felt a tingle run up his spine, and he sat back, his head against the wall. A few moments later, feeling a quiet peace he didn't understand, he read to the end of the underlined section:

"And they which heard it, being convicted by their own conscience, went out one by one, beginning at the eldest, even unto the last: and Jesus was left alone, and the woman standing in the midst.

When Jesus had lifted up Himself, and saw none but the woman, He said unto her,

"Woman, where are those thine accusers? Hath no man condemned thee?"

She said, "No man, Lord."

And Jesus said unto her, "Neither do I condemn thee: go and sin no more."

Avery sat in the silence of his lamp-lit room, while outside the world was dark and coyotes called back and forth across the valley. The lamp began to flicker, and Avery was roused from his reflection. The flame was burning too high and smoking up the glass chimney, so he turned down the wick, got to his feet and threw another log on the coals in the stove. As he had only one lamp lit, he carried it to the bedroom before blowing it out.

∾ ∾

The bawling had stopped, and the calves were grazing contentedly alongside the steers, but Avery decided to give them one more day to heal up before making his drive.

He rode in among them the following morning, circled the herd, and slowly gathered them into a bunch. After they were settled, he moved them up and down the canyon, and when he felt he had a handle on them, he opened the gate and let them out onto the open grassland. They ran and kicked for a short distance and then settled down to graze, eagerly working on the change of grass. After a few minutes, Avery gathered them and moved out toward the gap.

It was well into the afternoon when he sighted the Double Diamond buildings. His cattle were played out, so when he turned back the lead steer, they were more than willing to stop. Most of the calves lay down immediately, while some of the steers nibbled halfheartedly at the grass. Avery left them there, riding at a slow trot toward the buildings. He heard the ringing of a hammer on an anvil as he rode through a high rail gate and slowed to a walk.

The yard was divided into two very distinct sections, with a small creek serving as the boundary. On the west side was a no-nonsense working ranch, laid out in practical efficiency, with the main features being a big log barn and a long, sturdy bunkhouse. Together they formed a large L, both buildings facing in on a hard-packed dirt compound. Just this side of the barn was a series of smaller corrals, with a larger holding area directly to the rear.

Across the creek, the signs of a woman's touch were obvious. Behind a white picket fence, a two-story log house with green trim and shutters sat in the shelter of tall cottonwoods. Under the windows were flowerboxes, and a creeping vine climbed a lattice on the front porch. From the front gate, a stone walkway ran straight between two rose hedges to a delicate walking bridge that spanned the creek and dared to set foot in a man's domain.

Avery had just dismounted at the corral when a skinny young man with narrow shoulders and buckteeth came out of the barn leading a saddled horse. He stopped in surprise when he saw Avery, and said, "Howdy. I thought you was one of the boys bringin' in strays. I was just comin' out to help you. Who are you anyway?"

"Avery Carson, recently of Texas."

"Colby Armstead. I'm the bronc stomper around here—that and whatever else it takes to earn my keep. Did you find some of our cattle upriver?"

"No, these are my cattle."

"Your cattle!" Colby was incredulous. "Where's your outfit?"

Avery gestured with his thumb and said, "Out west," and then changed the subject. "Anyone else around?"

"The other boys are all combin' the high country south of here. The cows ain't comin' down, seein' as it's been so warm."

"How about Ball? Is he around?"

"Yup. That's him makin' the racket on the other side of the barn. He's doin' a reset on the team. I'll warn you, though, he's in foul humor."

Avery raised an eyebrow in question.

"His women folks is hostin' their annual Thanksgivin' Dance two days from tomorrow. He ain't crazy 'bout the idea."

"But it ain't Thanksgivin'," Avery said.

"No, you're right; it ain't at that. I guess back home in Kansas where they come from, Mrs. Ball always hosted a Thanksgivin' Dance. Trouble is, out here, there could be a foot of snow on the ground come Thanksgivin' an' folks all got a ways to travel. Anyway, what Mrs. Ball wants,

Mrs. Ball generally gets, so she just moved Thanksgivin' to the first weekend in November. Folks don't seem to mind, and a good time is had by all."

"Except for Mr. Ball," Avery said with a smile.

"Ah he usually warms up to it. He just don't like all the extra work, this bein' a busy time and all. Most folks stay over, so we gotta clean out the bunkhouse and move to the barn loft. Me, I don't mind none 'cause every girl for miles around shows up, and I like dancin'."

"Sounds like a good time," Avery said, warming up to the talkative young rider. "I'd like to have a talk with Ball, sour disposition and all."

"Come on. I'll introduce you to him and then duck and run."

Avery followed young Armstead around the front of the barn to where Ball was working at the blacksmith shop.

Hearing footsteps, Ball let go of the hind foot on the horse he was shoeing, straightened up, and wiped the sweat off his forehead. He looked from Avery to Armstead with questioning eyes but waited for Armstead to speak.

"Mr. Ball, this here's Avery Carson. He'd like to have a word with you."

True to his word, Armstead ducked out and headed back around the barn immediately following his introduction.

Avery stood and regarded Ball, while Ball studied him.

"Who are you?" Ball asked bluntly.

"Like the boy said, Avery Carson, recently of Texas."

A light of recognition touched Ball's eyes. "Ah, from Texas. So you're the card cheatin' gun slick that Sheriff Coleman ran out of town. I ain't hirin'."

Avery felt a hot anger fighting its way to the surface, but he bit his tongue. "I ain't lookin' for work," he said levelly. "I got some cattle to sell."

Ball looked surprised. "The only cattle in this country belong to me, the Box X, and the Slash 7. I reckon you don't rep for any of them outfits, so any cattle you got you stole. Now why would I want to buy stolen cattle?"

Avery's eyes smoldered, and the muscles on his jaw twitched. "Mister," he said in a quiet voice, pregnant with the threat of danger, "I ain't a thief, and I ain't a card cheat. If I'm the gun slick you say I am, you're pretty stupid, your crew bein' gone and all. Lucky for you, I ain't what you named me for. However, I ain't above teachin' a loudmouth bag of wind some manners."

Ball's eyes grew wide in disbelief and then were wiped clean by a hard and sudden anger. "Why you fiddle-footed saddle tramp! I'll—"

"Hi, Daddy. Oh hello, Mr. Carson. I wondered whose horse that was at the corral." Carol Ball came walking around the corner of the barn. She was wearing a pale blue dress, and her auburn hair was hanging over her shoulders in two thick braids. "Mom's just made a fresh pot of coffee, and I'm baking cookies and bread. See." She held up two flour-covered hands. "We thought you might need a break, Daddy. And Mr. Carson, why don't you join us?"

Avery shifted his weight back and forth from one

foot to another and then said, "Thank you, ma'am. I'm much obliged. I got some white-faced cattle out there on the grass that I gotta get to town, and I've a ways to go before dark."

"White-faced cattle?" Carol asked.

"Yes, ma'am. I just stopped in to see if your pa wanted to buy them. He ain't interested, so I best get movin'."

Carol looked from Avery to her father questioningly, "But Daddy," she said, "you've been saying over and over again that you wanted to pick up some white-faced bulls. Why wouldn't you be interested?"

"You run along now, sweetie," Ball said. "Mr. Carson and I have some business to discuss and then I'll be right in."

"Well then, discuss it over coffee and cookies," Carol said. Then turning to Avery she said sweetly, "Please, Mr. Carson. I insist."

Avery couldn't help but see the humor in the situation, and his anger was down to a quiet simmer. Thinking Ball would refuse, he said, "Only if it's okay with your pa."

"Well of course it's okay with Daddy. Let's go!" Carol turned and headed for the house and then looked over her shoulder and said, "Come on!"

Avery looked over at Ball, and though his eyes still smoldered, Avery could see he was a defeated man.

"Don't be gettin' no ideas about my girls," he said gruffly.

Avery looked at him surprised, "Girls?" he said. "You mean there's more like her?"

"No, thank heaven. Anne's quite manageable."

Avery smiled in spite of himself, and some of the anger left Ball's eyes.

"After you," Ball said, and they headed for the house.

∾ ∾

Feeling extremely uncomfortable, Avery entered the front door and removed his hat. The air was warm and laden with the homey smell of fresh bread.

Mrs. Ball glided through the kitchen door and extended a hand. "Well this is a pleasant surprise. Mr. Carson?"

"That's right, ma'am."

Mrs. Ball was a handsome woman, tall and regal-looking with hair just slightly duller than her daughter's.

"Just hang your hat on the hook there and come on into the kitchen," she said. "Albert, could you step out back and bring me in a little more stove wood?"

Avery could tell Ball was uncomfortable leaving him alone with his women folks, and he said just loud enough for him to hear, "Don't worry, Ball. I'll be on my best gun-totin' behavior."

"It's you I'm worried about," Ball muttered. "These girls can more than hold their own."

Ball stepped outside, and Avery, glancing through the door to his right, saw an unusually large sitting room furnished in an elegant fashion for the frontier. He was surprised to see an upright piano adorning the far wall, and he wondered how in heaven's name they'd managed to pack it all the way from Kansas. He then stepped through a door to his left and entered a spacious kitchen with more cupboards than he'd ever seen and a heavy wooden table at the center. Mrs. Ball was pouring coffee, and Carol Ball was taking cookies from the oven. Sitting at the table was the third Ball woman. She had dark brown hair and a pale complexion, and she rose to her feet as he entered, smiling shyly.

"Mr. Carson, this is Anne," Mrs. Ball said. "Anne, Mr. Carson."

"Howdy, ma'am."

"Just sit up to the table. Albert will be back in a minute. Till then, you'll have to make do with female company."

Avery sat down, feeling self-conscious, and it surprised him that he was actually looking forward to Ball's return.

Carol did not seem the least bit uncomfortable as she stood at his side and set a plate of cookies before him. "Gingerbread," she said. "My specialty."

"They smell great, ma'am. Thank you."

Carol sat down opposite him as her father came in and dropped a load of wood into the wood box. He took a seat at the head of the table as Carol asked, "So what brought you to Bow City, Mr. Carson?"

Avery waited till he'd swallowed and then said, "These are real good cookies, ma'am."

"My name's Carol, and thanks. What did bring you to Bow City?" she persisted.

"I come up the trail from Texas to Kansas with a herd

of cattle. Then I figured I'd like to see some new country, so I just drifted. Ended up in Bow City by accident I suppose."

"Is your lady friend back in Texas? If she is, I'd think you'd want to get back there."

"Carol!" Mrs. Ball scolded. "Mr. Carson, I must apologize. Lord knows we've tried to teach the girl some manners."

"Sorry, Mr. Carson," Carol apologized, "but I think it's a fair question. Emily told me you brought her some beautiful material and asked her to sew a dress for a special lady. I don't think she could be all that special if she's in Texas and you're up here."

"Mr. Carson, you need not answer, and Carol, would you please stop prying into other people's personal affairs," Mrs. Ball pleaded. "And I don't like you spending so much time with Mrs. Harper every time you're in town. You know what they say about her."

"Even if it is true, I don't care. I like her, and anyway, Mr. McFadden's the one who started all the talking, and I don't like him."

"Carol!"

"I don't like him either," Anne said, speaking for the first time. "I don't like how he looks at me."

"Good Lord, Anne, now you!"

"What do you mean, you don't like how he looks at you?" Ball asked seriously.

"I don't know, Daddy. I'm sorry I said anything. It's not polite."

Ball's eyes remained on Anne for a moment, dark and

thoughtful, and then he turned to Avery and asked in a quiet but meaningful voice, "So, how did a footloose gent like yourself end up ownin' some white-faced cattle?"

Avery met Ball's gaze, and said, "I don't own them. They belong to the CP, an' I've been left in charge."

"The CP? Never heard of it," Ball said, disbelieving.

"Didn't Sheriff Coleman tell you about the place I found?" Avery asked.

"He did say somethin' about you findin' some squatter's shack, but he never mentioned any cattle. I find it hard to believe someone could have been runnin' cattle up there without anyone else knowin' about it."

"Well, I got a small herd up the hill a ways. Nine two-year-old steers, an' thirty-two mixed calves. Them steers was branded some time ago, and as you know, I just drifted in a couple of weeks back, so that outfit had to be there before I got here."

"Calves, why calves? Who'd want to buy them?"

"I'm hopin' someone will," Avery said. "It's a small herd up there, and no doubt some of them heifer calves are out of mammas that were sired by their daddies, so I didn't want them bred back. There's two good-lookin' bull calves in the bunch, and seein' how white-faced cattle are in short supply, I figure I'll have some takers. Now if you'll excuse me, I got some miles to make. Thank you for the coffee and cookies, ladies. I'm much obliged."

As he stood to leave, Carol said. "You will be at the Thanksgiving Dance, won't you? It's this Friday night."

"Well, I ain't much of a dancer," Avery said noncommittally.

"That's fine. I can teach you."

"Carol! Heavenly days!"

"Thanks for the coffee," Ball said, getting to his feet. "I'll just step out and see Mr. Carson off."

Outside, Avery took the lead, and neither man spoke till they were across the walking bridge. Then Avery turned and waited for Ball to speak.

Ball took his time. "I don't know what to make of you Carson," he said honestly. He paused again as if trying to make up his mind. "I don't like you," he went on, "and maybe it's 'cause I can't help but think you're hidin' somethin'. A man with character don't just pick up and leave everythin' for no reason."

"You don't live in Kansas anymore," Avery said.

Ball looked at him and shook his head. He stared off in the distance for a moment and then looked back at Avery. "Let's go look at your cattle," he said.

CHAPTER TEN

It was late when Avery rode into town. Ball had been unable to hide his interest when he'd seen the cattle, and Avery guessed he'd been motivated as much by not wanting them to go to the Slash 7 or the Box X as anything else. They'd settled on a fair price, and by the time Avery had helped drive them to a pasture south of the buildings, most of the day had been spent.

The street was dark save for the light that spilled from the saloon window onto the backs of three saddled ponies waiting patiently at the hitching rail. The horse nearest to Avery turned its head and nickered softly. The only other sound was the footfalls of his tired horse.

The barn doors were closed, so he rode around the east end of the building and was surprised to see the dark outline of a stagecoach parked alongside the corral. He off saddled and turned his pony loose in a new pen, where several leggy horses were eating hay. After throwing his rig over a rail, he fumbled in the darkness and found the ladder to the loft. He crawled into some loose hay and was soon asleep.

Avery awoke with a start to the sound of voices on the street and was surprised at how late he'd slept. The hay he'd used for a blanket was doing little to ward off the chill of the morning, and because he'd skipped supper, his stomach was making plans. He got up, brushed his clothes clean, and climbed down the ladder, his muscles stiff and sore. He'd just stepped off the bottom rung when the back door of the barn swung open.

Wally Gibbs looked at him surprised. "You slept in the loft?" he asked.

"Yep. Got in late and there was no lights at the hotel."

"You should've stopped by my place. I ain't got an extra bed, but I could've found you some blankets."

"I don't know where you live," Avery said truthfully.

"I guess you don't. West end of town, three doors east of the church. Got my name on the front door. Next time, stop in. I don't care how late it is."

"Thanks, I might do that."

"I was just headin' over to grab some breakfast. Care to join me?" Wally asked.

Avery didn't answer. He was remembering the last time he'd eaten an early breakfast at the restaurant, and Emily Harper hadn't been there. He was awful hungry but also realized that, though he was reluctant to admit it, he was looking forward to seeing her. Instead he asked, "What time does the bank open?"

Wally looked at him, surprised. "Usually not till

nine o'clock," he replied. I reckon it'll be open early this mornin' though."

"Why's that?" Avery asked.

"Well, rumor has it that, when the stage came in last night, it was carryin' a strongbox full of gold. It's just a rumor, mind you, but it did pull in behind the bank, and it was bein' accompanied by three armed guards, so I suppose it's true. They're due to be here shortly to hitch up, and they made it clear they didn't need my help, so I ain't plannin' to stick around."

"Isn't this a bit out of the way for shippin' gold?" Avery asked.

"Well, the town's sure been talkin', and the way the talk goes—mind you, who knows if it's true?—, but they're sayin' the gold comes from some big strike north of here. Apparently, they sent a decoy loaded with a box of rocks over to Cheyenne and then sneaked out with this stage and are headed for Denver by roads less traveled. I suppose it could be true."

"Well, that's all very interestin', but I reckon it's none of our concern. I was wonderin', Wally, if you'd mind steppin' over to the bank with me before breakfast. I got some business needs doin', and I figure I'll need an impartial witness."

Wally looked at Avery with a puzzled expression and said, "Sure I could do that. What kinda business?"

"It's a long story. You can hear it when I explain it to the banker."

Voices out back caught their attention, and Avery and Gibbs turned to see a tall, heavily armed man walk through the open barn door toward them. Behind him, they could see another man slipping a bridle on a horse.

"Gettin' ready to head out?" Wally asked.

The man nodded, his mustached face serious, and Avery could see he was not happy. He glanced at Avery, and his eyes lingered for a moment. Then he looked back to Wally.

"That was the plan," he said in disgust. "The driver was up late drinkin' with the insurance man and some local cowboys. They're both still in bed hungover, and the insurance man is the one callin' the shots. Hopefully we'll be rolling shortly. Did he settle up with you last night?"

"He did," Wally responded. "We're just gonna step out for a bit, unless of course, you need me."

"No, we should be fine. Thanks."

Avery nodded a good-bye as they turned to leave, and the mustached rider responded in kind, his eyes hot and dark.

The bank was two doors down from the saloon, kitty corner from the sheriff's office. As Wally had predicted, it was open. A smooth-faced young man with a brand-new haircut met them at the counter.

"I'd like to open an account," Avery said.

"Yes, sir. We're always happy to welcome new customers. What is your name?"

"Avery Carson, but the account won't be in my name."

"Whose name will it be in, sir?"

"The CP Ranch."

"The CP Ranch," the teller repeated, and though it was a statement, it was almost a question.

"That's it," Avery said.

"And are you the owner, sir?"

"I'm the ranch manager, and I'll need signin' authority."

"I see. And you have the proper authorization from the CP owner I presume?"

"The owner's dead."

The young man looked up, startled and confused. Then he said apprehensively, "I'm afraid I don't understand."

"Well I know this ain't regular, but before I go explainin' everythin' to you, are you gonna be able to help me, or am I gonna have to explain it all over again to one of your superiors?"

The young man's pride was hurt, and he said with as much firmness as he could muster, "I'm sure I can help you, sir."

"Good. Well, I know you don't know me, so you might not take me for an honest man. That's why I brought Wally here along. Do you know Mr. Gibbs?"

"Yes, I know him. He's a valued customer at our bank."

"Good, 'cause I'm gonna open an account for the CP ranch, and I want him to have joint signin' authority. That way, I can't draw out any money or cash any checks on the account unless both of us sign. That way no one will think I'm stealin' from the rightful owners of the CP. You understand?"

"Yes, sir, I understand. That could be arranged quite simply. But who are the rightful owners of the CP?"

"Well, it's like this." Avery then went on to explain about his finding the ranch and its dead owner. He told about the cattle he'd found and what he'd done. It was the first Wally had heard of the cattle, and in the end, the account was set up as Avery had suggested, and Wally left for the restaurant while Avery stayed to sign a few papers. As he was leaving the bank, he met Emily Harper coming in.

She smiled at him pleasantly.

"Well, hello, Mr. Carson," she said. "I didn't know you were back in town."

"Howdy, ma'am. I rode in late last night, and seein' how there was no lights at the hotel, I slept in the barn loft."

Emily laughed, and Avery liked the sound of it.

"Really, Mr. Carson," she said, "you're a valued customer at the hotel. The front door's never locked, so I'm sure if you get in late again, you could just check the register and take a vacant room."

"Well that sounds good, ma'am. I've gone from bein' a worthless saddle tramp to a valued customer, both at the hotel, and now at the bank here."

Emily smiled. "I suppose that means you're sticking around for a while. Peter will be happy to hear it."

"How's he doin'? He ain't cut himself up too bad with that knife of his, has he?"

"Well he's carved up every stick and twig he can find,

and yes, he has managed to carve himself up a little as well, but that's how you learn I suppose."

Avery nodded. "Yes, ma'am. It seems that's the way this ol' world works. You just hope none of them cuts is deep ones."

Emily looked at Avery seriously. "You're a philosopher Mr. Carson," she said.

Avery wasn't sure what to say to that, and he stood a moment watching the street before he changed the subject. "I'm just headed over to the restaurant for a bite. Wally's waitin' for me."

"I'll see you there then. I start work shortly."

Avery didn't know what else to say, so he turned to go and then thought to himself that he should have said good-bye. He looked back, but Emily was already inside the bank. Turning, he almost bumped into two trail-hardened riders who were stepping up onto the boardwalk.

"Excuse me," Avery said.

The taller of the two men looked at him intently and then, after a brief pause, simply nodded and walked on past.

Avery started for the restaurant, but warning bells were ringing in his ears. He glanced back over his shoulder and saw that both men were entering the bank. With a sense of foreboding, he looked across the street. Sure enough, another man was leaning against the sheriff's office, watching the sparse early morning traffic. He couldn't be sure, but remembering the gold shipment, he knew there was a good chance.

Instead of heading for the restaurant, Avery angled across the street toward the saddle shop and, using a big, rangy chestnut as a shield, stepped up onto the boardwalk. Leaning on an awning post, he settled down to wait.

From where he stood, it was not hard to watch the bank across the street while still keeping an eye on the man in front of the sheriff's office. All at once, he knew for sure. A tall rider stood leaning on the wall of the hotel, and barely visible beneath the hem of his long coat, Avery could see the barrel of a rifle. He remembered then that the men from the stage were at the barn, and he understood. Reaching down slowly, he removed the leather thong from the hammer of his six-shooter, and then it hit him. Emily was in the bank!

Too late!

Three shots, almost on top of each other, ripped into the quiet morning, followed by a fourth shot, as the horses in front of the bank reared and pulled back. Reins snapped, and a big bay flipped over on his back, while another horse ran blindly into the side of a passing wagon. Avery saw the man at the sheriff's office draw his pistol as Sheriff Coleman burst through his door, racing past him to the chaos on the street.

"Coleman! Look out!" Avery screamed, palming his pistol and snapping a shot at the outlaw who was taking aim at the sheriff's back. Avery's gun boomed loud under the awning, and the man was slammed off balance, sending his shot high and wide.

Instinctively, Avery stepped down onto the street to put the horse at the hitching rail between himself and the man at the hotel. Coleman had spun back around and was raising his gun as Avery let go a second shot. The outlaw staggered back, tried to bring his gun to bear, and then collapsed in a heap on the boardwalk. The man at the hotel had opened up with his rifle, and Coleman's leg went out from under him. As the sheriff fell awkwardly to the ground, two men burst through the bank door, lacing the street with pistol shots.

Avery fired over the back of the terrified chestnut toward the hotel and then, crouching low, turned and snapped a shot at the outlaws who were trying to mount their horses. Coleman was shooting too, and one of the bandits staggered, went down, and then got up again as a fusillade of shots hammered out behind Avery. Splinters flew from the post beside him while Coleman crawled blindly for cover. Avery heard the chestnut grunt as it took a bullet, and the gelding staggered sideways, crashing into him and sending him sprawling into the street.

He rose to his knees, scrambling clear as the horse went down screaming. He saw the man at the hotel fire toward the barn and then turn and swing his rifle back to him. Avery had no cover and only one bullet left. He lurched to his feet and raced toward the outlaw, whose legs seemed to buckle as he raised his rifle. Avery reached the middle of the street and, lifting his pistol, took a quick step to the left as a bullet whipped past his head. As his foot came down, he fired, and the man was driven back against the hotel wall. He then pitched forward onto his face and lay still. The shooting had stopped, and a horse was pounding away down the street, a man clinging to its back. Another man lay twisted and awkward in front of the barn, and Sheriff Coleman was limping toward the bank, his pistol trained on a prostrate figure.

Emily!

Without bothering to holster his gun, Avery ran reckless, past shouting people, past the milling horses. He pushed a man aside and staggered drunkenly through the bank door. The room was thick with bitter smoke, and a man lay sprawled on the floor in a pool of blood. The young teller was on his knees, bent over him and shouting over his shoulder.

Avery looked frantically around the room, and then he saw her. She was sitting on the floor in the corner, her knees held tightly to her chest, her eye's wide with horror, fixed on the dying man a few feet away. Jamming his empty pistol into his holster, Avery fell to his knees and grabbed her face in his hands. "Emily!"

She looked into his eyes, and he saw that her face and the front of her dress were flecked with blood. He pulled her to him, and her body was stiff and rigid.

"Emily," he said again, and he scooped her up in his arms and carried her from the building.

Overhead, an unspoiled sky looked down on the carnage of the street. A pistol shot sounded, and Emily flinched, as someone put down the horse that had crashed into the wagon. She put her arms around Avery's neck and clung to him, her face in his chest.

"Carson, I need to have a word with you." It was Sheriff Coleman.

"Later," Avery said. Hearing footsteps, he turned to see Wally running toward him.

"Is she all right?" he asked.

"She ain't hurt as far as I can tell," Avery said, "but I don't think she's all right."

Wally looked at Emily, concern in his eyes. "Bring her to the hotel," he said.

Avery followed him and turned his shoulder awkwardly as he went through the hotel door, trying to shield the dead outlaw from Emily's view. Wally looked at the registry.

"Room four's empty. Upstairs."

Avery carried Emily to the stairs while Wally disappeared inside the restaurant.

She lifted her head from his shoulder and said, "I'm sorry, Avery. I'm okay now. You can put me down."

"We're almost there," he said.

"It was awful." Emily's voice was barely louder than a whisper.

Avery laid her on the bed, and the way she looked up at him made his heart hurt. He heard footsteps on the stairs and turned to see the short, middle-aged waitress come through the door with Wally close behind.

"How is she?" the lady asked in a gruff but not unfriendly voice.

"I'm okay, Miriam," Emily said, making an effort to get off the bed.

"Nonsense, young lady. You just lay back down and rest while I get you cleaned up. Have you got something you could change into while I wash that dress?"

"At home in my bedroom," Emily said meekly.

"I'll go and fetch it," Avery volunteered.

"Could you look in on Peter?" Emily asked.

"Sure. We'll bring him by once they've cleaned up the street a little. You know where he's stayin', don't you, Wally?"

"Sure. At widow Conklin's."

"Me and Wally'll look after things, ma'am," Avery said. "Don't you worry 'bout nothin'."

"Thank you. Thank you so much."

∽ ∽

Two men were throwing the limp body of the dead outlaw into the back of a wagon when Avery and Wally stepped back onto the street.

Wally glanced at the bloodstained boardwalk, then turned to Avery and said, "You did some shootin', didn't you?"

"I reckon so," Avery said, his face grim. "That reminds me, I ain't reloaded."

Wally watched sober faced as Avery drew his Peacemaker and began shucking out empty cartridges. "I've never seen anythin' like it," he said. "I don't reckon that goes for you."

"I'm afraid not Wally. But I hope this was the last."

"I was sittin' in the restaurant about to order breakfast when all hell broke loose. First I hit the floor, and if I was smart, I would've stayed there. I was curious 'bout what was goin' on though, so like a fool I crawled over and sneaked a peek over the window ledge. I was just in time to see you chargin' across the street straight at the fella with the rifle. Then you stopped and stood there like a soldier on parade with bullets flyin' past your ears …" Wally shook his head and sighed deeply, looking off down the street. When he looked back to Avery, his face was troubled. "I thought you was a dead man, Avery," he said.

"I had no choice. I only had one bullet left, and it was too far for good pistol shootin'."

Wally looked at Avery and shook his head again. "For a fella I consider to be my best friend, I sure don't know a lot about you," he said.

"Avery Carson, recently of Texas. I spent five years as a peace officer with the Rangers. I seen more trouble than I care to remember."

Wally watched Avery close the loading gate on his pistol and shove it back into his holster. Their eyes met, and he said, "Thanks for tellin' me. I was just wonderin' how you got so expert, that's all. I'll head over to widow Conklin's and check up on young Peter, and you can go fetch the dress."

CHAPTER ELEVEN

Bow City's main street was a beehive of activity as Avery made his way back west along the boardwalk. Sheriff Coleman, who was directing traffic, spied him and came hobbling over.

Avery stopped and waited for his approach. "I thought you caught one, Sheriff," he said.

"No, I'm okay. A bullet took off my boot heel and kind of twisted my ankle; that's all."

Avery nodded, and the two men stood for a moment regarding each other.

Avery could tell Coleman's mind was full of questions, but in the end all he said was, "I guess you saved my life, Carson."

"It was a close thing, all right. I'm glad it didn't go worse."

"Thanks."

Avery nodded and, after a brief pause asked, "One of them outlaws got away?"

Coleman nodded that he had. "I thought about

throwing a posse together to go after him, but there's a lot to do here, and he didn't get any of the gold."

"It's just as well, I'd say. No use anyone else dyin'. Who was the fella in the bank?"

"One of the armed guards. I guess there were four of them, and they'd always let on that there were three. They kept one man hidden in the stage and with the gold at all times. He slept in the bank I guess."

"They musta been pretty sure somethin' was up," Avery said.

"I think they must have. Anyway, Carson, they're down to two riders, and the insurance man wants to know if he can hire you for the rest of the trip to Denver. He's at the bank now. His name's Simpson."

"I ain't interested," Avery said. "I got an errand to run, but I'll be at the hotel later if you need me."

"When I see him, I'll tell him." Coleman turned to leave and then, shaking his head, turned back to Avery and said, "You know, it's a miracle no town folks were killed."

"I'd say so," Avery agreed.

Not wishing to speak to anyone, Avery took the next space between buildings and made his way to the side street. When he got to the Harper house, he noticed again that the front gate needed a new set of hinges, and he made a mental note to do something about it. He paused at the front door and couldn't help but feel he was trespassing. Though he knew no one was home, he knocked softly before entering.

The house was small, sparsely furnished, but clean.

He was standing in a crowded kitchen area with a wood stove, a scarred table, and three chairs that didn't match. Immediately to his left was a small pantry and, straight ahead, an open door leading to a sitting room. Avery walked across the kitchen and saw that Emily used the adjoining room for a work area. Her sewing machine sat beneath the south window, and draped over the back of a worn leather chair were several pieces of green cloth. A door on the east wall of the sitting room led to the house's only bedroom. It was open, and Avery stepped inside.

Two single beds sat against the walls on opposite sides of the room with a narrow walkway between them. On the wall at the foot of each bed was a set of hooks where clothes hung. Over Peter's bed was a pair of overalls and two shirts. Hanging from the hooks at Emily's bed were three dresses. Only one hung from a clothes hanger, and it was the silky green dress she was sewing.

Avery crossed the room slowly and admired it. He didn't know much about dresses, but it looked finished to him, and it looked beautiful. He was tempted to bring that one to Emily, but he knew it wouldn't do. One of the other dresses was gray like what he'd always seen her wear, and the second was light blue with a small pattern of darker blue flowers. Avery took that one off the hook, and as he turned to go, he caught the fresh, clean feminine smell of the fabric, and all at once he was remembering Audrey. It brought him up short, and he stood still a moment, gently caressing the soft cloth between his thumb and forefinger, staring at the delicate pattern without really seeing it. A heavy sigh escaped from deep within his chest, and then he stepped quickly out the door and headed for the hotel.

He took the side street back, and because most of the activity was in front of the bank, he was able to enter the hotel unseen. Emily's door was closed, so he knocked hesitantly.

"Who is it?" It was Emily's voice.

"It's me, Avery."

"Come on in."

Emily was sitting up in bed. Her hair was down, and she was wearing a flannel night gown that he guessed Miriam had found for her. Her hands were folded on the blankets in front of her, and she smiled almost shyly as Avery entered.

She watched him lay the dress on the foot of her bed and then pull up a chair and sit down facing her.

"I feel rather silly," Emily said.

"Why's that?" Avery asked.

"There's nothing wrong with me, and everyone's falling all over themselves trying to help me. The only reason I couldn't go to work is because Miriam's washing my dress, and I couldn't very well go in a nightgown."

"You ain't silly, ma'am, and I'm just glad you ain't hurt."

Emily smiled and bit her lip. "I was so scared," she said. Then in a fragile voice, looking down at her hands, she continued. "The last time I saw someone killed it was my mother. Nothing was the same after that."

Avery wasn't sure what to say. He wanted to offer comfort, but nothing seemed good enough. Once again, his own loss found its way to the surface of his thoughts, and he knew that words would always be too small. They sat in silence while a sleepy fly buzzed against the windowpane and voices sounded on the street below. After a time, Avery cleared his throat and said, "I'm sorry, ma'am. Peter told me about you losin' your folks."

Emily looked up at him. "Did you see Peter?" she asked.

"Wally went to fetch him. I went for the dress."

"Thanks for that. I suppose I could get up and go to work now, even if it is my Sunday dress."

"Sorry, ma'am. I just thought it was pretty."

"Oh please, there's no need to be sorry," Emily said quickly. Then smiling, she continued, "Thank you, Mr. Carson, I think it's pretty too." After a pause while she fussed with the edge of her blanket, she spoke again. "I guess you saw that I've almost finished the dress you ordered. I just have to do the hemline."

"Yeah I saw it, and I think it's beautiful. You musta got right to it. I didn't expect it would be done near so quick. Where did you learn to sew like that?"

"I lived with my aunt for a while. She was a seamstress, and I learned from her."

Avery could tell it wasn't a pleasant memory.

Emily smiled at him, but her eyes still seemed sad. "Now we just have to hope your Emily likes it," she said.

"I hope she will. I ain't quite figured out how to give it to her yet, and she ain't exactly 'my Emily.'"

Emily looked as if she was about to say something else but then decided against it.

Avery got up from his chair. "Well, ma'am," he said, "I missed supper last night and breakfast this mornin'. My stomach's sure startin' to complain about it, so how about I go downstairs and order us a late breakfast. If you're up to it, you can join me downstairs. Or if you like, I can bring it up here. Wally and Peter should be along pretty quick, and they can join us."

"You don't have to buy me breakfast, Mr. Carson. And anyway, Peter and I ate earlier."

"Well you can call yours dinner, and I'll call mine breakfast, and unless you ain't up to eatin', the only question is where you want to have it."

Emily smiled and said softly, "I can join you downstairs. I've never actually been served in the restaurant before. And thank you, Mr. Carson, you are a kind man."

Avery shuffled his feet, feeling suddenly self-conscious. "Well, ma'am, I don't know about that," he said. "I do know, if I don't eat pretty quick, you're gonna see what kinda man I am. I'm apt to get grumpy."

ༀ   ༀ

Avery was glad that the restaurant was almost empty. It was too late for breakfast and too early for dinner, and no doubt, most of the men who were not otherwise occupied were gathered at the saloon, and there would be plenty to talk about. He took his usual seat, and the short lady named Miriam came over to his table.

"How is she?" she asked.

"She's perked up a bit I reckon. She's worried 'cause

she ain't at work, but I told her to come down once she was dressed, and I would buy her dinner. You figure the boss will be okay with that?"

Miriam scowled at Avery and said, "I am the boss, and of course it's okay. No one's been in here since the big gunfight. It'll probably get real busy in about an hour though, but if she ain't up to it, I can handle things."

"Thanks, ma'am."

"She's a good girl that one. I don't care what anybody says. Now what can I bring you?"

"Maybe just a couple of coffees for now. I ain't sure what she'll want, and I may as well order at the same time. Wally and her boy should be showin' up anytime too."

Emily came through the door just as Miriam was returning with the coffee. She'd done her hair in a loose braid, and Avery thought she looked fresh, clean, and beautiful in her Sunday dress. She looked apprehensively at Miriam and said. "I'm okay to start work now if you need me. I'm sorry I was such a bother."

"You just sit down there and rest. If you're up to it, I could use some help when the noon rush comes."

Emily smiled her thanks, and Avery got to his feet as she took a chair opposite him. The light through the window seemed to make a halo over her pale hair, and it struck Avery that she had an angelic quality to her beauty that was a rare thing. He was suddenly at a loss for anything to say, and they sat in comfortable silence while they sipped their coffee.

The quiet was interrupted when Miriam came bustling over to their table. "Well, what would you like?

The chickens are laying real good, so I have lots of eggs today."

"I reckon I'll have steak and eggs then, ma'am," Avery said.

Miriam turned to Emily, and Emily said, "That sounds good. I'll have the same thing please."

Miriam nodded, glanced out the widow, and said brusquely, "I wonder how the events of this morning will affect the big shindig Mrs. Ball is throwing."

She turned and hurried off to the kitchen, and Avery looked at Emily and asked, "You plannin' on goin' to the Thanksgivin' Dance?"

Emily looked down at her coffee and waited a moment before answering. She shook her head slowly and, without looking up, said, "No. I don't think so. For one thing, I have no way out and back."

"I could borrow a wagon from Wally," Avery offered. "I'll drive you and Peter out if you'd like. There's likely a bunch of kids goin', and I'm sure he'd have fun tearin' around."

Emily smiled. "I'm sure he would," she said. She waited a moment; made as if to speak; hesitated again; and then, speaking apprehensively, said, "Mr. Carson, you may have heard some of the rumors about me. There are people in Bow City who threatened to boycott this restaurant if Miriam didn't let me go. Maybe I'm a coward, or maybe I'm too full of self-pity, but I'm not sure if I'm welcome at the Ball house, and I'm too proud to ask. A lot of people would like it better if Peter and I just moved away."

"Well Mrs. Harper, I sure ain't one of them, and I know Carol ain't either."

Emily looked up quickly at his use of Carol's first name, but he didn't notice.

"I can see it might be hard, and I won't twist your arm," he continued, "but it might be good for you to go. I'm sure you'd be welcome at the Ball house."

"Do you go there often?" Emily asked.

"No, I've just been there once. I sold Albert a few head of cattle."

"Wally told me about the place you found. I suppose they are your closest neighbors."

Miriam brought their food to the table, and Avery thanked her. They ate in silence, but now it was an awkward silence, and Avery had no idea why. He was wondering what was keeping Wally and Peter when Emily spoke.

"Maybe I will go," she said. "What can it hurt, really? If you can get a wagon, and don't mind Peter and me tagging along, we'll come."

Avery's face lit up. "I'd be honored to take you, ma'am. It'll be fun for Peter too, I'm sure."

"I must confess it makes me a little nervous. I haven't been to a dance since I was a little girl, and then all I did was twirl around and watch my dress billow out."

"I ain't much of a dancer myself," Avery said, trying to reassure her. "Carol told me she'd teach me some steps, so I'm sure she'd help you out too if you want some pointers."

Just then Wally and Peter came through the restaurant

door. "Here's Peter and Wally now," Avery said. He moved over next to the wall to make room at the table, and Emily did the same. Wally and Peter took their seats, and Peter stared at Avery wide-eyed but said nothing.

"Sorry I was so slow, ma'am," Wally said. "I wanted to make sure things were cleaned up outside."

"Thank you, Mr. Gibbs. That was thoughtful of you," Emily said. Turning to Peter, she tousled his hair and said, "Am I glad to see you! Mr. Carson and Mr. Gibbs are going to spoil you with all this restaurant food."

"Did you hear the shooting, Ma?"

Emily's face became serious. "Yes I did," she said, "and I'm just glad to see you safe."

Peter turned to Avery and asked, "Are you a gunfighter, Mr. Carson? Timmy McFadden said his pa knew you were a gunfighter the first time he saw you. He said it was lucky for Sheriff Coleman that you were here."

Avery shifted in his seat uncomfortably. Emily's eyes were on him, and he shot a hot glance Wally's way.

"Sorry, Avery. I shoulda taken the side street," Wally said.

Avery turned to Peter. "I ain't a gunfighter, Peter. Mostly fightin' is somethin' you want to avoid. Sometimes, though, you can't, and a man has it to do; that's all. Let's not talk about it, okay?"

"That's because there is a lady present, right?"

"That's right, son," Avery said.

॰॰ ॰॰

Avery and Emily waited while Peter and Wally finished up their meal. Miriam came and cleared their dishes, and they were just about to leave, when several people passed by the window. Avery heard them enter the hotel, and then Sheriff Coleman came into the room followed by a cluster of men. Before taking a seat, he caught Avery's eye, turned, and said something to the man directly behind him.

The man he'd spoken to was tall and slender and wore a broadcloth suit. He glanced Avery's way and then came over to their table, acknowledging Emily with a nod of his head. "Hello, madam." Then turning to Avery he said, "Mr. Carson, allow me to introduce myself. Randall Simpson, from Claiborne Insurance. First off, I want to thank you for helping to save our gold shipment."

As of yet, Emily had no idea what part Avery had played in the events of the day, and she looked quickly his way with a startled expression.

Simpson continued speaking. "As chief officer in charge of this shipment, I am entitled to give out reward money as I see fit, and as I and the company are greatly indebted to you, I have already made out a check for that purpose. Sheriff Coleman gave me your name, and I hope I have not erred in the spelling." He placed a check for two hundred dollars on the table.

Glancing at it, Avery said, "That's how it's spelt."

"You are quite the pistol fighter, Mr. Carson."

"Mr. Simpson, this ain't the time or place," Avery said firmly.

"We don't talk about fighting when there's a lady present," Peter piped in.

Simpson smiled at him and said, "Cute." Then he turned to Avery. "Unfortunately, I do not have the luxury of choosing another time and place. I am down two guards, and I need to move this shipment quickly. I am asking, Mr. Carson, if you would consider accompanying us the rest of the way to Denver. If you would, I will double that." He gestured to the check on the table.

"Sorry, Mr. Simpson. I have a previous commitment."

"Triple."

"No. I wish you better luck on the rest of your trip."

"We still have all the gold, Mr. Carson."

"And two less guards to pay. I guess it's your lucky day."

A suggestion of anger crossed Simpson's face, and he said, "Good day, sir." Nodding to Emily, he said, "Madam." Then he turned and left.

"I'm sorry about that, Mrs. Harper," Avery said.

"That's all right," she responded, her face serious. "Peter already told me about you being a Ranger. I understand it is sometimes necessary to possess certain skills. I wish it wasn't so, but I know the world can be a hard place. Every day, I try to remember to thank God for the good things. It helps me to see them."

"Now you're the philosopher," Avery said.

Emily smiled a sad smile. "This morning was a long time ago, wasn't it, Mr. Carson. I'm so glad you weren't hurt."

CHAPTER TWELVE

Things were different for Avery in Bow City. He was no longer invisible, and he wasn't sure he liked it. Being a footloose saddle tramp had its advantages, as no one had any expectations. Now he was something of a celebrity. Some people looked up to him; some people were afraid of him. But everyone was curious. If he avoided them, as was his natural tendency, his reputation as a dark, mysterious gunman was reinforced. If he went against his nature and made a point of talking with strangers who were hungry for information, he'd have to rehash over and over things he'd just as soon not talk about.

He tried to walk the line by making eye contact and acknowledging the greetings of passing strangers, while still keeping to himself as much as possible. It was an uncomfortable situation, but he was beginning to realize that the more one shut out the world, the smaller his world became, and if he was going to live in the area, he'd need to embrace the community.

The day before the Thanksgiving Dance was one of

preparation. It seemed that most of the town's citizens would be attending, and Avery wondered how the Balls would accommodate everyone. Apparently, the Double Diamond provided the beef, and everything else was potluck. Apparently as well, the Double Diamond bunkhouse was about three times the size needed to accommodate its crew, as Albert Ball was a planner with big plans. As a result, he had ample room for the late-night hangers-on to stay over.

Wally was able to provide Avery with an old spring wagon and a team, and he also sent along a stack of blankets in case the weather took a turn for the worse. Avery threw an ax and some dry firewood into the box just to be on the safe side.

By early afternoon, he was running out of things to do, so he stopped in at the mercantile and picked up a new set of hinges and some lag screws for the Harpers' gate.

Peter was playing in the front yard and ran to meet him as he approached. "Hi, Mr. Carson," he said excitedly. "Ma's making cookies to take to the dance!"

"I can smell them from here," Avery said. "Figure she'd let us try a couple?"

"I already asked her, and she said no. She's afraid there won't be enough. She let me lick out the bowl though."

"And you never saved any for me?"

"I never knew you were coming, Mr. Carson, or I would have."

Avery laughed. "That's fine, Peter. I don't think I'll starve just yet. I'm gonna see if I can't fix this here saggy gate. Want to give me a hand?"

"Sure, what do you want me to do?"

Avery dug in his hip pocket for a couple of wrenches and handed them to Peter.

"Here," he said. "See which one of these fits on them lag screws there."

Peter took the wrenches, and the first one he tried was the right size. He immediately gave it a turn and the wrench slipped off.

"You gotta turn it back the other way, son. If you don't, you'll just be makin' it tighter. Here, let me get it started, and when I get tired, you can spell me off."

Avery backed the screw out until it was turning easily and then handed the wrench to Peter. With great concentration and determination, Peter struggled with the wrench till he had the screw out. He handed it to Avery, a look of triumph on his face.

"Well that worked real fine," Avery said. "How about I get the next one started, and then you can finish it off too."

The process was repeated till the first hinge was off.

"Here, Peter," Avery said. "Now I'm gonna need you to hold the gate upright like this. Otherwise, she's gonna want to tip over now that we got the first hinge off, and then somethin's liable to break."

"Okay, Mr. Carson. And if you get tired turning the wrench, we can trade off."

"Sure thanks. That sounds like a good plan."

After taking turns with the wrench, the gate was finally free. Avery was laying it flat on the ground when the door to the house swung open.

"Hello, Mr. Carson," Emily said as she stepped outside. She was carrying a plate of cookies. "Thanks for doing something about that troublesome gate."

Avery waved in an offhand manner. "Not a problem, Mrs. Harper. I was just runnin' out of things to do; that's all."

"Well thanks just the same," she said, brushing a loose strand of hair from her forehead with the back of her hand. "I thought maybe you and Peter had worked up an appetite, so I brought you some cookies."

Peter was about to say something, but Avery cut him off. "Thanks, ma'am. We've sure been smellin' them, and there's nothin' like fresh bakin'."

Peter didn't see any reason to chance a turnaround in his good fortune, so he gratefully took a couple of cookies and politely thanked his mother.

"I'd like to offer you some lemonade or something, but all I've got in the house is water," Emily said.

Avery swallowed, "Water would be fine, ma'am. These are real good cookies."

Emily smiled appreciatively, "Gingerbread," she said. "My specialty. I'll get you each a glass of water."

She turned for the house, and when she'd stepped inside Peter said, "These are good cookies, aren't they, Mr. Carson."

"Boy, I'll say."

"Do you like my ma, Mr. Carson?"

"I think your ma is a fine lady."

Peter smiled. "Me too," he said. "I figure she must

really like you 'cause I know she likes me, and she wouldn't give me any cookies."

Emily came out with the water, and after Avery and Peter had had a drink, she watched as they hung the gate. When they'd finished, it swung freely, and Peter was obviously proud of the accomplishment.

"Look, Ma!" he said. "Look how easy it swings!"

Emily laughed. "That's great Peter. You and Mr. Carson did a real fine job."

"You got the afternoon off?" Avery asked.

Emily nodded. "John Macy—he owns the Slash 7—well he has a spinster sister that's moved in with them. Miriam's training her today, and she'll be working one or two days a week."

"Are you worried about job security?" Avery asked.

Emily smiled and shook her head no. "Miriam needs help some mornings, and now if it gets busy, she'll call me and send word out to the Slash 7 for Grace to cover the afternoons. Grace doesn't really need the money. She just wants to get out some and have something to do."

There followed a time of silence while Peter busied himself with opening and closing the gate. Avery wondered if he should excuse himself and leave, but he didn't want to. Emily didn't seem to want to leave either, or maybe she was just being polite and waiting for him to go. He glanced at her at the exact same moment that she turned to look at him and their eyes met briefly. Emily smiled uncertainly and then looked quickly away, and Avery thought he saw a hint of color coming into her cheeks. He felt the urge to reach out and touch her face. He wanted to tell her that she was beautiful, that the pretty green dress hanging in her bedroom was for her, and that she could wear it to the dance if she wanted to. Instead he swallowed and said nothing.

"Oh no! My cookies!"

Emily turned and fled through the front door. Avery could hear her banging around in the kitchen, and he and Peter turned and looked at each other in the pregnant silence that followed.

"Oh, they're ruined!" came the mournful cry through the open door.

Avery didn't know if he should duck and run, stay where he was, or go into the house and try to offer some consolation. He wasn't allowed in the house on account of Emily's nosy neighbor, and he didn't want to leave without trying to do something, so he waited.

It wasn't a long wait. Emily came and stood in the doorway, a look of anguish and disappointment on her face. She slumped against the door frame and said in a defeated voice, "I burned the cookies. Now there's nowhere near enough."

"Can we eat the burned ones, Ma?"

Emily smiled in spite of herself and said, "Oh, Peter, all you think about is your stomach."

"Beggin' your pardon, ma'am," Avery said, "but that's an important thing for us men to think about. I reckon Peter got right to the point and asked a fair question."

Emily dropped her hands to her side and shook her head in resignation.

"We may as well do something with them. Come on

in, Mr. Carson, and I'll put the coffee on. Maybe that'll help them go down easier."

"What about your neighbor?" Avery asked, motioning with his head toward the house next door.

"I don't care what she thinks right now," Emily said. "Come in, and don't mind the mess or the smoke."

Avery and Peter entered the house and took a seat at the table while Emily wiped it off with a dishcloth. As she leaned over to open the widow behind the table, Avery said, "Oh no, ma'am, don't be doin' that."

"Why not?" Emily asked, turning to face him.

"Well, you let all this smoke outside, and every Indian in the territory's gonna think you're sendin' up a signal invitin' them for coffee an' cookies."

Before Avery had a chance to move, Emily fired the dishrag at him, hitting him square in the face.

"Well, thank you kindly, ma'am," he said with a smile. "I always like to wash up a might before I eat. Here, Peter, why don't you wash up too."

Peter smiled and took the dishrag. He didn't say anything, but he kept looking from his mother back to Avery. Emily went to the counter and began cutting the burned edges off several cookies.

"This is so disappointing," she said. "I hate to go to the dance empty-handed."

"Is there time to make some more?" Avery asked.

Emily turned and faced him. "I'm out of flour," she said apologetically, "and I can't really afford to buy anymore right now."

"I'll go pick some up if you'd like to bake some more," Avery offered.

"Thank you, Mr. Carson, but you've been so kind to us already. I hate to be a burden."

"Nonsense, ma'am. I'd like to do it. You'll recall I run into unexpected riches with that reward money. You tell me what you need, and I'll run over and pick it up. I need to get to the bank anyway to open my own account."

Emily bit her bottom lip and thought a moment. Then she sighed heavily. "All right," she said, "and thank you." She hesitated a moment and then reluctantly added, "I'm out of molasses and short on sugar too."

Avery smiled at her, and she smiled back, and nothing more was said about it.

CHAPTER THIRTEEN

The grand exodus from Bow City began shortly after noon the following day. The warm weather was hanging on, and the blue sky above smiled down on a festive atmosphere. Avery and company headed out around two in the afternoon. Peter wanted to show his mother where they'd gone fishing, and Emily didn't want to arrive too early. Though she didn't say it, Avery knew she was a bit apprehensive about her reception and wanted things to be in full swing when they pulled in. He'd also agreed to head back that evening, even though it would be late. From the talk around town, Avery had gathered that a number of people did this rather than spend the night in a crowded bunkhouse.

The trip out was enjoyable. They took time to throw stones in the pool below the falls, and Avery promised Peter an overnight camping trip the following summer. As the Double Diamond buildings came into view, however, Emily grew quiet. Avery didn't know what to say to reassure her, so he said nothing. As they drove into the yard, he could hear the sound of fiddle music, and he saw that a big bonfire had been built in the compound in front of the barn. Children were running in and out of groups of adults scattered hit and miss around the yard, and a few couples danced and twirled to a one-man band sitting on a stump by the fire. Rigs were parked all along the lane way, and the corral beside the barn was a mass of horse flesh.

"I'll just pull up to the barn and drop you two off and then turn around and find a place to park this thing," Avery said.

"Oh I don't mind walking," Emily responded. "Let's just pull in behind that buggy there."

Avery looked at her and said, "It'll be all right. No one's gonna bite you. Just have fun okay?"

Emily looked at him and asked, "Does it really show that much?"

Avery smiled at her but didn't answer. Instead he said, "Your hair looks really nice the way you made it curly like that."

She looked down at her hands on her lap and then glanced back up at him. "Thank you," she said.

They lapsed into silence as Avery drove into the yard. Peter stood behind them in the wagon box, holding onto the back of the seat and taking in all the activity with excited anticipation.

As Avery pulled to a stop, Carol Ball stepped off the walking bridge and came straight toward them. She was wearing an elegant purple dress that complemented both her auburn hair and her willowy figure, without seeming the least bit inappropriate. She approached them with an unrehearsed grace and charm that was so unspoiled and spontaneous, it was refreshing. Her face radiated the excitement she was feeling as she greeted them. "Hello, Emily and Peter! I'm so glad you came!" She turned and acknowledged Avery with a mischievous smile and said. "Mr. Carson, I hope you haven't forgotten your dancing lessons."

Avery smiled awkwardly, climbed from the wagon and turned to help Emily down. "Peter," he said, "want to hand them cookies and dishes down?"

"Oh Emily," Carol said. "I just love the dress you made me. It's perfect!" She turned around so that Avery and Emily could admire the fit from the back and then turned to face them. "What do you think?" she asked.

"You look beautiful, Carol," Emily said graciously. "I don't think you can help it though."

Carol giggled. "Oh here, let me take those cookies," she said. "Oh gingerbread! I know Mr. Carson likes Gingerbread cookies, don't you, Mr. Carson? Here, Emily, come with me. We'll take them to the house. That's where the food will be served. Because it's so nice out and so many people came, we're going to have the main dance outside, and Mom and my sister and I will take turns playing the piano inside. People can dance and visit in there too." Then becoming instantly more serious, she turned to Avery and said, "Oh, Mr., Carson I almost forgot. You're something of a celebrity in Bow City now. Everyone's talking about it."

Avery shifted uncomfortably from one foot to the

other and said a little too gruffly, "Well I don't want to talk about it, ma'am."

Carol was not offended. "No of course not, I'm sorry. I just want to warn you, though; Daddy doesn't think he likes you. He says he knew you were a gunfighter and that we don't need your type around here. Mother pointed out to him that Bow City did need you around, and he didn't know what to say to that. Daddy sometimes comes across as a grumpy old bear, but we girls know better. Please, don't let it bother you. He'll come around."

Avery couldn't help feeling uncomfortable, and if it wasn't for Emily and Peter, he'd have just as soon headed for the safe quiet of the gap. He just nodded and in a flat, even voice said, "Thank you, ma'am. I'll keep it in mind."

Carol smiled, took Emily by the elbow, and then turned and waved over her shoulder as they stepped up onto the bridge. Avery watched them go, his thoughts with Emily as she headed for uncharted waters. Her Sunday dress looked tired and shabby next to Carol's, and his heart went out to her.

"Hey, Peter! Come on! We're buildin' a fort in the hayloft!" The speaker was a towheaded boy about Peter's age, and Peter looked at Avery as if asking permission.

"Better get to it, son. I'll come and see what you're buildin' once I've unhitched the team."

Peter ran off with the other boy, and Avery climbed up into the wagon.

ॐ   ॐ

After unhitching, Avery tied the team to a couple of vacant posts at the corral. He watched them for a moment to make sure they wouldn't cause trouble with the horses next to them, and when all seemed quiet, he took a stroll behind the barn. Ball had done a fine job laying things out, and Avery couldn't help but respect him for it. The barn itself was built from big pine logs and was better put together than a lot of houses he'd seen. He could hear the boys playing in the loft, and remembering his promise to Peter and feeling responsible since Emily had left Peter with him, he climbed a ladder in an empty stall.

The loft was about three-quarters full of hay, and several bedrolls were stacked against the front wall. The boys were roughhousing on the empty floor space, and when Peter saw Avery, he came running over.

"I take it you ain't buildin' a fort," Avery said to him.

"No we're playing king of the castle! I was king for a while, but Sam and Timmy knocked me off!"

"Well that sounds like fun," Avery said.

"It is, but I'm getting real hungry."

Avery laughed. "I reckon they'll be callin' us for supper shortly," he said. "I'll come and get you when they do."

Avery turned to go, but Peter stopped him. "Mr. Carson," he said. "What's a whore?"

Avery felt a cold knot in his stomach. "Why do you ask, Peter?"

"Timmy McFadden said that Ma was a whore. I didn't know what it met, but I told him she wasn't."

Avery felt a smoldering anger growing in his chest, but he kept his voice calm. "Well, Peter, it's a bad thing to call someone a whore. I reckon Timmy don't know what it means, or he wouldn't have said it." Avery stopped and thought for a moment, and he hoped he wasn't making a mistake. "Peter," he said. "I want to talk to you man to man, okay?"

"Sure, Mr. Carson," Peter said, eyeing him seriously.

"Let's step on down the ladder where it's a little more quiet. I'm sure it's almost time to eat anyway."

Peter followed Avery down the ladder and then waited expectantly for him to speak.

"Now, Peter, this here's just between you and me, okay?"

Peter nodded.

"First, I don't want you to say anythin' to your ma about what that boy said. It might upset her, and you bein' the man around the house, you need to try and make sure that don't happen. Understand?"

"Yes, sir."

"Now mosta the time fightin' ain't a good idea, and if someone calls you a bad name, you might be best to just shake it off and forget about it. They're probably just stupid and can't help it anyway, so don't let it bother you. But the way I see it, if someone says somethin' nasty about someone you love, like your ma or your sister if you had one, don't wait around. Just up and smack 'em right in the mouth where them nasty words came from. It don't

138

matter if the other fella's bigger 'n you, and it don't matter if you gotta take a lickin'. You just got it to do; that's all. A fat lip or a shiner will heal up pretty quick, but sayin' mean things can hurt for a real long time. That's why I don't want you talkin' to your ma about it. You and me know that Timmy don't have the slightest idea what he's talkin' about, but your ma might not know that. You understand what I'm sayin', Peter?"

"Yes, sir."

The loud clanging of the dinner bell interrupted their conversation, and Avery put a hand on Peter's shoulder. "Maybe let it go this time, Peter. And no matter what, have some fun. It ain't every day you get to go to a Thanksgivin' Dance."

∽ ∽

The crowd was slowly making its way across the bridge to the house when Peter and Avery left the barn. They found themselves at the tail end of the line on the way to two long tables on the veranda. Both were loaded with food. The man in front of Avery turned around at his approach, and Avery knew he'd seen him before but couldn't place him.

The man nodded a greeting to Avery, and extended a hand. "John Macy," he said.

Avery shook the man's hand. "Avery Carson, recently of Texas."

Putting a hand on the shoulder of the woman in front

139

of him, Macy said, "Mr. Carson, this is my wife, Beth. And this is my sister, Grace."

The two women turned and greeted him, and Avery said to the older of the two women. "I hear you'll be workin' some at the restaurant, ma'am."

"Well word does travel fast in a small town. Yes, I'll be filling in now and then. How did you know?"

"Mrs. Harper mentioned it to me. She's the other lady that works there. That's her comin' now."

"Yes, I've met Emily," Grace said as they watched her approach.

Emily's pace quickened when she saw them. "Mr. Carson, Peter, there you are," she said as she drew near.

Avery watched for a hint of how things had been going, but her manner gave nothing away. "I have our plates here," she said, sounding a bit out of breath. "Oh, hello, Grace. How did it go yesterday?"

"Well it went all right I suppose. I only spilled coffee on one gentleman."

Everyone shared a chuckle, and then Macy turned to Avery. "I hear you brought some white-faced cattle into the country," he said.

"Well, I can't take credit for that. I am lookin' after some though."

"Albert told me about the place you found. Strange we never met the man."

"I find it mighty curious myself," Avery agreed. "I asked Sheriff Coleman to look into the CP brand for me. I'm hopin' we can track down the fella's next of kin."

"I'm guessing Coleman's been a little busy lately with the goings-on in town."

Avery nodded and said, "That's a fact." He was relieved that Macy never brought up his part in the gun battle, and he wondered if he knew. He also realized that the two Macy women had been in quiet conversation and had not included Emily. He wondered at it and thought it was probably nothing. Turning to Emily, who was standing at his elbow, he asked, "How's it goin'?"

"That's a big house," she said, noncommittally. Then looking up at him with a light in her eyes she said, "I can't believe they have a piano!"

"Yeah, I seen it," Avery said. He noticed the shine leave her eyes, and he wondered why. "They musta had a time gettin' it up here. Plenty of hills and river crossin's I'm guessin'." Because of her apparent interest, he asked, "Do you play the piano?"

Emily didn't answer immediately. Then she said, "I played a little when I was a girl. My mother taught me—mostly hymns from church. She would play the left hand, and I'd play the right. It's been a long time, but I loved it."

They were almost to the steps of the house, and Avery was thinking about what Emily had said.

"I guess that's what I like most about these get-togethers," he said. "The music. Seems like I don't get to hear it near often enough. Mind you, the food ain't too bad either."

Emily smiled at him and then looked down at Peter.

"I think that will be Peter's favorite part. What have you been up to, young man?"

"We were playing king of the castle in the barn loft, but right now, I can't wait to eat!"

They loaded up their plates, and when they got to the end of the first table, Albert Ball was slicing meat from a large roast. He served Emily and Peter with no comment, and as his eyes met Avery's, Avery said, "Albert. I ain't sure if you've met Mrs. Harper here and her son, Peter. Mrs. Harper's the lady who made your daughter that pretty dress."

Ball smiled politely at Emily and then at Peter. "Mrs. Harper, Peter, I'm glad you could come. Carol sure likes her dress, ma'am, so thank you."

"Your daughter is a beautiful lady, Mr. Ball. I think she would look good in any dress she wore, but you're very welcome. It was my pleasure."

Ball turned to Avery and said, almost begrudgingly, "I butchered one of those steers you sold me. I think it's the best beef I've ever eaten."

"I'm lookin' forward to tryin' some," Avery said. "If you need any more breedin' stock, let me know. I'd be interested in swappin' a few heifers with you, as I'd like to get fresh blood into the herd."

Ball paused a moment while he studied Avery, his knife halfway through the roast. Then he nodded curtly and said, "We could talk about that sometime. I might be interested."

The second table was full of desserts, and Avery saw Emily's cookies on the corner nearest to him.

"I guess we'll have to come back for the sweets later," he said as he snatched a cookie from the plate and took a bite.

Peter watched him and asked, "Can I have one too?"

"Peter," Emily scolded, "It'll spoil your supper."

Avery looked at the food on his plate and said, "Ma'am, I don't think that'd be possible," and handed Peter a cookie.

"Emily and Peter!" Carol was standing in the doorway. "It's a bit crowded in here, but come on in. I saved you a couple of spots at the table."

Emily turned to look at Avery.

"You go on in," he said. "I'll go find a spot on the grass where I ain't far from the sweets."

Peter followed his mother inside, and Avery looked for a secluded spot where he could eat and wouldn't have to talk to anyone. He walked around the south side of the house, sat down, and enjoyed the best Bow City's cooks had to offer. After a good sampling of sweets, he rinsed his plate in the creek and took it back down to the wagon.

The daylight was slipping away, and Avery could see sparks from the fire dancing skyward to be lost against the painted clouds of a glorious sunset. He made his way to the fire and stood with a circle of watchers as couples danced a two-step to a lively fiddle tune. The fiddle player was the barkeep from the saloon, and another man was serving drinks from the back of a wagon.

As in most frontier communities, women were in short supply, and, looking around, he guessed the four who were dancing were the only ones present. Emily and the Ball girls were still up at the house, and Avery figured that a large percentage of the female population had taken their meals there.

The music stopped, and as partners were being traded, the fat lady from the mercantile walked straight toward him. Before he had a chance to shrink into the darkness, she grabbed his arm and said, "Come on, you Texas gunslinger. Don't be shy!"

Avery found himself being drug out into the firelight, and as the music started up, he had no choice but to dance. He felt himself being muscled around the circle, and he did his best to keep time.

"You're a good dancer, Texas! My but this is fun, isn't it!"

"Yes, ma'am."

They danced around the circle a couple of more times, and the fat lady seemed to be getting short of breath.

"My name's Mabel McFadden. My husband doesn't like to dance much, but I'll twist his arm later when he's had a couple of drinks." She laughed at her own joke and then said, "Most folks just call you that Texas gunfighter. I never did catch your name."

"I'm sorry, ma'am. Avery Carson."

"I was glad to see you brought that pretty little woman from the restaurant out here. It's the first time she's come."

Avery didn't say anything, but he wondered what was coming next.

"She's a good girl that one. I know my husband isn't too fond of her, but that's where we disagree. I tend to think highly of any woman who's a good mother, and she's a good mother. Lord knows, I wish my little Timmy had her son's manners."

A smattering of applause sounded, and Avery turned to see several women coming across the walking bridge.

"Oh darn," Mabel McFadden said. "Here come all the pretty women. Now I won't be near so popular!" Again she laughed, and as the music stopped she said, "We're glad to have you in Bow City, Mr. Carson."

"Thank you, ma'am. Thanks for the dance."

Avery made his way to the edge of the circle. All of the women were quickly paired up, and he noticed Emily was dancing with the skinny young hand he'd met the first time he'd been to the Double Diamond. He remembered the boy had said he liked dancing, and it was no wonder. He was obviously good at it.

He decided to get a drink, and as he neared the wagon he hesitated. There, standing by the rear wheel, was a tight group of riders, and three of them were the Slash 7 boys from the poker game. Crazy Nick spotted him first and said something to Staples, who turned and eyed him with a watery gaze.

"Howdy, Texas," he said.

"Howdy, Staples. Nice evenin', ain't it?"

"Lots of pretty ladies, that's for sure."

Avery ordered a beer and was digging in his pocket for some money when Staples said, "Me an' the boys here was wonderin' what kinda fighter you'd be without that pistol there."

Avery turned and regarded Staples, who was standing

feet apart and swaying a little. "Who would I be fightin'?" he asked.

"Why me, I reckon," Staples said.

Avery pretended to take a moment to size him up and then he said, "You got pretty beefy shoulders there, Staples. I think I'd probably take a lickin'."

"You better believe you would, Mr. Texas."

Avery touched his hat and said, "Be seein' you boys."

The cowboys mumbled their response, and Avery caught Carnes's eye. Carnes smiled knowingly and touched the brim of his hat.

Back at the edge of the firelight, Avery stood and watched the dancers. Emily was paired up with a weathered old cowhand, and Carol was dancing with Sheriff Coleman. Several boys, including Peter, were holding sticks to the coals and then waving them in circles and figure eights once they'd caught fire. Avery smiled thinking that, if their mothers weren't so taken up with the dancing, they'd soon put an end to the fun.

The music stopped, and Carol, ignoring several offers, walked toward him. "If you won't choose me, I'll have to choose you," she said.

Avery hesitated and then set his drink on the ground inside the circle of watchers and rose to take the arm Carol offered. The fiddle player slowed things down to a waltz, and Carol smiled up at him as they danced at the edge of the firelight.

"You're a terrible liar, Mr. Carson," she said playfully. "You're a good dancer."

"I'd say you're the terrible liar, ma'am, but thanks."

"Are you having fun?"

"Yes, ma'am. It's good of your family to put this thing on."

"Did Daddy try and bite your head off?"

"No, ma'am. He was very civil."

"I'm glad to hear it. I want you to feel like you can stop in anytime."

When the music ended, Avery thanked Carol and then looked around for Emily. She was at the fire taking Peter's stick away. As she straightened up, Avery was at her side.

"Could I have this dance, ma'am?" he asked.

Emily let go of Peter's stick, turned quickly, and brushed a loose strand of hair from her face.

"Why, yes, Mr. Carson," she said, smoothing her skirts self-consciously.

As Avery guided her away from the fire, he noticed that Peter had his stick back in the coals. He was hoping for another waltz, but the fiddle player struck up a two-step, and the dancing area became so crowded he had a hard time guiding Emily around without running into someone.

"Are you havin' a good time, ma'am?" he asked.

"I'm having a wonderful time, Mr. Carson. I'm so glad we came."

"It's sure a beautiful night. Hard to believe it's November."

"Oh no. Peter's back playing in the fire."

"I reckon he'll be fine, ma'am. At least he'll live till this dance is over."

"I'm sorry, Mr. Carson. I probably worry too much. I don't want to be an overprotective mother. Do you think I'm an overprotective mother?"

"No, ma'am. I think you're doin' a fine job with that boy."

Emily paused a moment and then said, "Thank you. It means a lot to me that you like him."

They danced the rest of the dance in silence. When the music stopped, Avery thanked her, and she was immediately claimed by the skinny young puncher, while he made his way back to the sidelines. It didn't look as if Carol or Emily was going to get many breaks, and after a couple of more tunes had been played, Avery asked Mabel McFadden for another dance. After that, he danced with a young lady who was the daughter of the Box X foreman.

A few dances later, Carol came and claimed him again, and as the music ended, Anne stepped in to inform her that it was her turn to play the piano up at the house.

"Oh darn," Carol said. Then she turned to Avery and said, "Come up to the house if you like. There's food and refreshments in the kitchen."

Avery noticed Emily standing off in the shadows as if she were waiting to speak to him, and he guessed it was time to head back to Bow City.

"I don't know. Miss Ball," he said. "I think it might be time for us to head for town. It'll be gettin' awful late for young Peter." He slowly made his way to the edge of the circle where Emily waited, and Carol and Anne walked beside him.

"You mean you're not staying over?" Carol asked.

"No, ma'am."

Carol glanced at Emily and then turned to Anne and said, "Tell Mother I'll be right up." Then looking back to Avery she said, "Just one more dance. Okay?"

"Is that all right, ma'am?" he asked, looking at Emily.

"Of course, Mr. Carson. We don't have to leave unless you want to. Peter will sleep on the way home anyway."

Carol looked again at Emily and smiled. Then she said to Avery, "I'll be right back."

She walked quickly over to the fiddle player, bent over close, and said something in his ear. He nodded while continuing to play. Carol came back to Avery; she held out her arm, and he took it. The music stopped and there was a brief pause; then the fiddle began to play a slow, melodic, and haunting waltz. As they danced, Carol slid her hand around to Avery's back, drawing herself close, her face inches from his chest. Nothing was said during the entire dance, and as the last notes sounded, Carol pulled slowly back, sliding her hand down Avery's arm and letting it linger for a moment on his sleeve before taking it away.

"I'll look forward to your visits," she said and then turned and walked into the darkness.

CHAPTER FOURTEEN

A very stood where he was and watched Carol walk away. His heart was beating fast, and he didn't want it to be. He drew a deep breath and blew it out and then walked over to where Emily waited. He felt awkward and off balance and had trouble looking her in the eye.

"We can go now, ma'am," he said.

"I'll go find Peter," Emily said in a detached voice.

No one said anything on the way over to the wagon, and Peter shuffled along slowly at his mother's side, obviously played out. The darkness was deep away from the fire, but presently their eyes adjusted, and the black shape of their wagon loomed before them.

"I'll need to go get the team," Avery explained needlessly.

"All right, I'll make a bed for Peter."

Avery helped Emily into the wagon box and then handed Peter up to her.

"There you go, young fella. Did you have fun?"

"Yes, Mr. Carson," Peter said sleepily. "I even danced with a girl."

So did I, Avery thought to himself, and he shook his head subconsciously. "I'll be right back," he said, but Emily was already fussing with the blankets, and he wasn't sure she heard.

He turned and walked toward the barn, his head swimming. That dance with Carol had really thrown him off. He hadn't seen it coming, but Carol had told him as plain as a woman could that she wanted him to be her man. He admitted somewhat reluctantly that she was a very attractive woman, and that her body so close to his had been unsettling. *Why did Emily have to see it! What could I have done, push Carol away?* He stopped in mid stride as another thought came to him. *Did I even want to?* Confused, he shook his head and moved out again.

He had just reached the corral when a drunken voice came out of the darkness. "Well look at you. First you got Miss Ball fallin' all over you, and now you get to drive the pretty little whore home."

It was McFadden, and without thought, Avery dove forward, driving a big hard fist square into the man's face. It landed with a sickening splat, and McFadden staggered backward, his arms windmilling. He slammed into the corral rails and then pitched forward, collapsing like a rag to the ground where he lay, unmoving.

Avery stood feet apart, looking down at him and sucking in big breaths of air. Then as clear as the sunrise in the morning, he knew for sure. He was in love with Emily Harper.

"I got some work to do," he said out loud.

〰   〰

Emily was sitting alone on the wagon seat, a blanket over her shoulders when he returned. The team was fidgety and fresh after standing for so long, and hitching them up in the dark was a bit of a struggle. When he'd finished, he climbed up on the wagon and saw that Emily had laid out his warm jacket for him.

"Thanks, ma'am," he said, as he shrugged into it. "It's sure cooled off a might. Are you gonna be warm enough?"

"I should be fine, thanks."

Emily sat stiff and rigged, staring straight ahead while Avery settled down beside her. She moved ever so slightly to the outside edge of the seat to give him room as he took hold of the lines.

"Is the little fella already asleep?" Avery asked, glancing over his shoulder.

"Yes. It didn't take long. It was a big day for him."

The trace chains jingled and the steel rims clattered as the wagon lurched into motion and Avery swung the team around in a wide circle. The sky was a blanket of stars, and the silver-tipped mountains to the north and west showed that the moon would soon be rising. They rode in silence for a few minutes, and then Avery said, "You're powerful quiet, ma'am."

"I'm just tired; that's all."

"It's been a long day, all right."

Again they rode in silence, swaying back and forth with the rhythm of the trail, serenaded by the hooves on the road and the creaking of the wagon. A full moon began cresting the horizon and the grass ahead shone in its light.

"That's sure pretty, ain't it," Avery volunteered.

"It's beautiful," Emily agreed.

The trail dipped down into shadows, and Avery could hear the sound of running water. He let the horses have a drink and then clucked them into motion, splashed across the river, and climbed the opposite bank back into moonlight.

"Is somethin' wrong, Mrs. Harper? You're awful quiet."

"You're not talking either."

"Well, you see, ma'am, that ain't unusual. I'm quiet most of the time. I guess you wouldn't know that 'cause around you I can get to be a blabbermouth—you and Wally; you both seem to have that effect on me."

"Maybe I'm quiet most of the time too," Emily said.

"Well I guess that could be. I like to hear you talk though. Tell me what you're thinkin'."

"Please don't ask."

Avery felt suddenly stupid and unsure of himself. "Sorry, ma'am," he mumbled. "I guess I'm bein' kinda' nosy."

Emily was quiet a while longer, and then she turned to Avery and said, "No, I'm sorry, Mr. Carson. Sometimes I just fool myself into thinking things could be different;

that's all. I had a good day, and thank you for talking me into going. It was a great day for Peter too."

Avery hesitated a moment and then summoned his courage and turned to face her. "What do you mean, things could be different?" he asked.

"Please, Mr. Carson," she said softly, "I have my secrets, and I think its best they stay that way."

Avery waited a minute before speaking, not sure how to proceed. The moon was now showing itself completely and the stars faded in its light.

"Do you remember the first time I met you?" he asked.

"Yes. I've thought about it often, and I'm terribly sorry."

Again he turned to look at her. "Sorry? Whatever for?"

"I spoke unkindly to you. Don't you remember?"

"Ma'am, I ain't holdin' that against you. I was thinkin' about what I did. Do you remember that?"

"Sort of."

"Well I just want you to know that the reason I acted like I did, was 'cause I thought you were the most beautiful woman I'd ever seen, and I was mad at myself for noticin'."

Emily looked up at him startled and then looked away.

"I'm glad you think I'm beautiful, Mr. Carson," she said, "but that almost makes it worse."

Avery wondered at her comment, but said nothing. Finally he said, "This is gonna take a little tellin', ma'am, and like I said, most of the time, I'm a man of few words. I'd like for you to know though."

"All right. I like to hear you talk too."

Avery paused a moment and then sighed heavily and said, "A little better than a year ago, I was a married man, Mrs. Harper. My wife and unborn child were killed when I sent her to town with a half-broke team. Well just before town, the road turns and then crosses a bridge over the river. She was almost to town, and everythin' was fine till the train pullin' out of the station blew its whistle. The team spooked and ran away on her, and they never quite made the corner. The buggy tipped over and smashed into the side of the bridge before spillin' into the river. One horse was killed outright, and the other one had two broken legs and had to be put down. Of course the worst of it I already told you.

"I was runnin' away when I came to Bow City, ma'am. I didn't want to see no one or talk to no one. Maybe I thought that my bein' miserable was sorta payin' for my mistake. I don't know. Anyway, noticin' a pretty girl didn't really fit with my program of self-pity."

Emily looked at Avery, her eyes full of compassion. She placed a hand on his arm and said, "I'm so sorry, Mr. Carson. I had no idea."

"It's all right, ma'am. There's another thing I want to tell you, and I'm sorta stickin' my neck out here, but I got it to do I reckon."

Avery paused, needing to muster the courage to continue, and Emily waited, curious but apprehensive.

Finally, looking straight ahead, Avery said, "I wish

that last dance I had tonight woulda been with you instead of with Carol."

Avery heard Emily's startled gasp, but when she didn't say anything, he said, "I hope you ain't angry, ma'am."

"No. I'm not angry." Then in a voice soft and fragile she added, "I wish it had been me too."

Avery felt hope surge in his heart, and he turned to her and said, "How's about I stop the team right here, and we can step down and have that dance?"

Emily paused a moment before answering. "Mr. Carson," she said, "that would be lovely beyond my dreams, but it's no good. It would just make it worse."

"That's the second time tonight that you said that, ma'am. I don't see why—"

"Mr. Carson, I'm not a good woman. If you knew the truth about my past, you'd want nothing to do with me, and I would be doing you a grave injustice to play with your affections just because I desire them, while all the time hiding the truth from you. It's hopeless."

Avery was quiet for a while, and he could hear that Emily was crying softly and trying to hide it from him.

"Ma'am," he said gently, "When I came to this country, I thought my life was over. Like it or not though, my heart kept beatin' and the sun kept comin' up in the mornin'. Now thanks to you an' Peter, I don't want it to be over. What went on in the past will always be there, and I sure enough think about it from time to time, but I read in the Bible a few days back that God's mercies are new every mornin'. I also read about a woman with a past that most folks couldn't tolerate. Jesus didn't condemn her though. He told her to go and sin no more, and I reckon that's what you're tryin' to do. I know it can't be easy to change things when folks try to keep you right where you are, but …" Avery sighed heavily and shook his head. "I'm sorry, ma'am. Here I am blabbin' on and on again, and if I stuck my big nose where it don't belong, I hope you'll forgive me. You can keep your secrets if you like, Mrs. Harper, but if them secrets is what keep us apart, I sure wish they didn't have to be secrets."

The wagon springs creaked and the steel rims rattled over stones on the trail while the moon hung big on the horizon.

"I'm scared," Emily said.

"Please don't be."

Emily sighed deeply, and then her voice trembled when she spoke. "My name isn't Mrs. Harper, and I've never been married." She glanced quickly Avery's way and then looked straight ahead, sniffed, and wiped her nose. She was silent for a moment, but when she spoke again, her voice was stronger. "Peter doesn't know. I've lied to him too. My name is Emily Olson. My parents were good people, and when things changed in my life, I didn't want to bring dishonor to their name." She paused, and Avery knew this wasn't easy for her, but then she continued. "After the Indian massacre, I went to live with my aunt and uncle because there was no one else. I was twelve years old at the time. We moved a lot, and their home was nothing like ours. My uncle was a heavy drinker, and my aunt seemed sad all the time. She was a seamstress as I've told you, and Uncle Carl only worked off and on."

Here Emily paused again, and Avery could tell she was growing uncomfortable. He didn't say anything, however, but wondered if he should.

Then she spoke again. "When I was fourteen, my uncle came to my room one night while I was sleeping …" Emily stopped speaking, and Avery could hear that she was crying again.

Without thought, he put his arm around her shoulders and drew her to him. "It's all right, Emily," he said. "You don't have to do this."

"No, I want to. I'll be okay. Is Peter still sleeping?"

Avery took his arm from her shoulders, pulled the team to a stop, and turned around to look at Peter. It was hard to see him in the darkness, but with the wagon and the team standing still, he could hear the boy's even breathing. "I reckon he's sound asleep, ma'am."

Avery clucked the horses back into motion, and Emily wiped her eyes and nose and continued speaking. "My aunt knew. She didn't say anything, but she knew. I felt so ashamed and dirty, and I couldn't look her in the eye. When my uncle left the next morning, she gave me some money; I think it was all she had. I ran away. The next stage out of town was going west, so that's the way I went. I was so scared, and I felt like everyone was looking at me and that they knew. I got a job waiting tables in Ogallala, and I had a room upstairs. It was okay for a while, but then one evening, while I was cleaning up the dishes, Mr. Cranston came in. He was the owner of the restaurant. I could tell by the way he was watching me that he wanted the same thing my uncle had. I left some dishes in the sink so he would think I was coming back and went upstairs to my room.

"I had some money I'd saved in a drawer by my bed, and I took it. I heard him climbing the stairs, so I quickly opened my window and climbed out onto the porch roof. I heard him hollering as I jumped down into the alley. I ran and had no idea where I was going, but when I reached the edge of town, I saw some campfires from an immigrant train. I hid in one of their wagons, and they didn't find me till the following afternoon.

"They left me at the next town, and I got a job looking after three children for a rancher who had an ailing wife. I stayed there for almost two years, and they were good to me. His wife died, though, and he moved back east to be with family. I took another job at a restaurant, and the same thing happened; only I didn't get away in time. I stole some money and ran away again.

"I ended up in Denver, where I met Mike O'Donnell. He owned a gambling house and was a wealthy man. He made me an offer, and I was tired of running and of trying to protect what I'd already lost. I agreed to his offer. I had money, a good house to live in, fine clothes, and I was safe. Everyone was scared of Mike, and at first, he was good to me. Then I got pregnant. He blamed me, and things changed. He beat me a couple of times, and I think he hoped I'd lose the baby. I didn't though, and when Peter was born, I was happier than I'd been in years. I didn't have to go to The High Roller anymore. That had been part of the bargain; I was to deal faro every night at his casino. Anyway, he said I was no good to him anymore until I got my figure back.

"I knew I had to get away. I wanted Peter to grow up in a good home, and I didn't want him to know what kind of woman I was. I was afraid though, because I didn't want to be alone again, and Mike offered a security of sorts. I ended up going back to The High Roller, and Mike was happy because his take was better. When I was working, I had to leave Peter with an elderly woman who worked for Mike as a cleaning lady.

"When Peter was two, I took him to church on Christmas Eve. I hadn't been to church since I'd worked for the rancher and his wife, and I was afraid because I didn't want people to recognize me. I sat in the back row, and the singing and the candle light ..." Emily turned to face Avery, and the moonlight turned the tears that rimmed her eyes to diamonds. "It was beautiful," she said wistfully. Looking down at her hands folded on her lap she continued. "I remembered being a little girl and how good it was, and I knew this was what I needed for Peter. The preacher read from the Bible about when God sent an angel to Joseph to warn him, and because of it, they were able to escape with the baby Jesus. I prayed to God that He would help me and my baby escape. I asked Him to please send an angel. You might think that sounds silly, but it didn't seem silly at the time.

"I left the church, and I was almost home when I met Mike. He was looking for me and was extremely angry because I was supposed to be at The High Roller. He hit me and knocked me down in the snow right in front of

Peter. Peter started crying, and when I tried to go to him, Mike kicked me. He said he was through with me and that I was going to have to start earning my living like all his other girls.

"Just then a stranger stepped out of the darkness and told Mike to leave me alone. I recognized him as a man I'd seen at the church. He said, 'Don't you know it's Christmas?' Mike swore at him and told him Christmas was just another day and to mind his own business. They got in a fight, and Mike who never lost a fight, was getting the worst of it. I saw Mike pull a knife from inside his coat, and I screamed for the man to look out. The next thing I knew Mike was lying in the snow, his face all bloody, and the stranger was standing over him holding a gun. There was no shot, so I think he must have hit him with it.

"He took Peter's hand and said, 'Come with me.' I followed him, and he put us on the stage. He gave me some money and told me to go where they'd least suspect. His last words to me were, 'Don't ever go back.' He rode beside the stage till we were well out of town. Then he pulled up and waved good-bye, and I never saw him again. He was my angel, and God heard my prayer. I was running away when I came to Bow City too."

Emily finished speaking, and Avery didn't say anything. Ahead, he saw a small poplar bluff beside the trail, and as he pulled alongside it, he reined in the team and looked at Emily. "I'll be right back," he said.

Stepping down from the wagon, he walked forward, took the lead shank off the hames of the near horse and tied it to a tree. He then walked back to the wagon and, looking up at Emily said, "Miss Emily Olson, if you'd give me your hand so I can help you down, I'd be most honored if you would have a dance with me."

Emily's breath caught, and she hesitated a moment. Then she stood and came over to Avery's side of the wagon, took the hand he offered, gathered her skirts, and stepped onto the wheel hub. Avery put two strong hands on her waist and lowered her gently to the ground. Emily didn't say anything, but her breathing was shallow and her heart was pounding. Avery took her elbow and guided her from the shadows of the trees to where the moon bathed the grass, and they danced.

CHAPTER FIFTEEN

A very wished the drive home could have been longer. He'd put another blanket over Peter and draped his jacket over Emily's shoulders. They sat together on the wagon seat, a heavy blanket over their laps, and another over their shoulders.

The lights of Bow City showed ahead, and Avery said, "I'm surprised there's still lights burnin' this time of night. I reckon it must be folks that headed back before us."

"You're not planning on sleeping in the loft again, are you?" Emily asked.

Avery smiled. "No, hopefully there's a room available at the hotel." The horses picked up their pace, and Avery had to rein them in for fear of waking Peter. "I guess you figured out by now that you sewed yourself a dress," he continued. "I hope you like it."

Emily lifted her head from Avery's shoulder. "I was beginning to wonder," she said. "Why did you do that?"

"I don't know. For some reason, I felt the need to look out for you an' Peter after I met you in the store. Honestly,

I wasn't tryin' to win you over. I didn't even know if I'd be stickin' around this part of the country back then."

"Well, thank you, Avery. It's the nicest gift anyone's ever given me. Once I got to know you, I started feeling jealous of your Emily. I would try the dress on, and it was so beautiful ..."

Avery couldn't make out Emily's features, as a small wispy cloud had drifted across the moon. When she continued speaking, however, her voice was soft and full of emotion.

"Now I can't believe that your Emily is me."

Avery waited a moment, and then said, "I thought of givin' it to you for the dance, but I wasn't sure how to go about it. I thought you might think I was chasin' you, and I wasn't sure if you wanted to be chased. Do you wish you woulda had it?"

Emily didn't answer right away. Then she said, "I'm ashamed to admit I was thinking less than charitable thoughts when I saw Carol looking so wonderful. She's done nothing but be a good, honest friend to me, but when it was so obvious she was chasing you, I was wishing I'd sewn a less flattering dress."

"I had no idea," Avery said honestly. "That one really snuck up on me."

Emily smiled and shook her head. "I don't think she could have been more obvious. I don't blame her though, so I can't be angry. Yes, I sort of wish I would have had the dress but ... I'm a little bit nervous to wear it."

"Why's that?"

"It's not quite as modest a dress as what I'm used to

wearing. With all the talk and with my past, well, I might feel a little self-conscious."

"Well, ma'am, that sounds very interestin'. I can't wait to see it on you."

Emily was quiet for a while. Then she said in a tentative voice, "Avery, when I kissed you while we were dancing ..." She shifted her weight uncomfortably, and then continued hesitantly. Well, I've never kissed a man because I wanted to before. I'm a little afraid of how I'll do with that too."

Avery thought a moment about what she'd said, and then, with his voice full of feeling, he responded. "Miss Emily, all I know is that, if you're agreeable to it, from here on in, I'd like to make lookin' out for you an' Peter my full-time job—for as long as we both shall live."

Emily clutched Avery's arm beneath the blanket, put her face against his shoulder and said quietly, as if for fear of waking from a dream, "I would like that very much."

Avery drew a deep breath and let it out. It was as if he were too small to take in the enormity of what was happening, and he struggled with what to say that could do it justice. The warmth of Emily's body snuggled close to him seemed to make him bigger and smaller at the same time. Part of him rose to the challenge of the new and beautiful purpose that now lay before him, and another part was afraid he'd be too small to give all he wanted to give. He paused, trying to figure out how best to say what he wanted to say. "Emily," he said after a time, "please don't worry about all that other stuff. I'm thrilled just to be with you, and I hope I can make you feel honored and cherished and make up for some of them things that never shoulda happened. One thing I can promise you, though, is that I'm gonna be a hard man to get rid of."

Emily's grip tightened on his arm. Avery could feel his shirt sleeve getting wet, and his heart had never felt so full.

Most of the lights in town were out when he pulled the wagon up in front of the Harper house. For a while, neither of them moved, and then Avery said, "I guess for Peter's sake and everyone else's, you're still Mrs. Harper."

"Do you think that's best?" Emily asked.

Avery thought a moment before answering. "I see no reason to confuse the little fella," he said thoughtfully. "Maybe bein' right ain't always right. Yeah, I think that'd be best; for now anyway." He waited a moment, and then stepped down and helped Emily from the wagon. She watched as he jumped up in the box and picked Peter up in his arms. The boy stirred in his sleep but never woke up.

"Do you want to hand him down to me?" Emily whispered.

"I'm all right I think," Avery whispered back. He climbed down from the wagon box as carefully as possible, and Emily went ahead and opened the door. He stood in the doorway while she lit a lamp and then he followed her to the bedroom.

Emily pulled back the covers on Peter's bed, and Avery gently laid him down and tucked the blankets in around him. Emily stood back watching, her eyes full of emotion.

Avery looked down at Peter and then turned to go, but Emily was blocking his way, and she didn't move. She stood up on her tiptoes, and her kiss on his lips was soft and gentle. She stepped back and whispered, "I love you, Avery Carson."

Avery reached out and touched her cheek. "I love you too, precious Emily," he whispered back.

He followed her from the room, and when she stopped in the kitchen, he said, "I better go. I was a married man once, and protectin' your honor might prove more difficult than I thought."

Emily smiled and said, "Being a loving wife might prove easier than I thought. Good night, Avery. Thanks for the best day of my life."

"Good night. I'll see you in the mornin'."

❧ ❧

Avery left town the following afternoon with a heart full of life, and his horse took to the trail as if he shared the feeling. He and Emily had talked, and they were going to get married the Sunday before Christmas, as the circuit preacher would be in Bow City for a couple of weeks. Avery had been reluctant to leave her, but had a long list of things he wanted to get done before the wedding. He was going to try to get an addition built on the cabin, and he hoped the good weather would hold. As he rode past the Double Diamond buildings, he remembered his dance with Carol. *I guess she'll hear about it sooner or later,* he thought.

෪ ෪

The day's light had all but faded from the sky when he got home, but he was up early the next morning, skidding logs from the nearby slopes. By late afternoon, he was busy with the broadax squaring timbers.

The following morning, he fashioned a crude stone boat using one of the first timbers he'd made and began dragging flat slabs of sandstone down from the canyon to use for a foundation. In the days that followed, he alternated between squaring timbers and laying stones. It was grueling work, but he threw himself into it with abandon. When a week had passed, he had a twelve-by-fourteen foundation jutting off from the kitchen side of the cabin, and about half enough logs squared.

It was early Saturday, just before sunrise when he saddled up and headed back to Bow City.

He was reluctant to do so, but as he neared the Double Diamond buildings, he drew rein and then headed for the yard. He tied his horse at the corrals and exchanged greetings with a wiry old hand he'd seen at the dance. He was told the boss was up at the house, so he crossed the walking bridge, mounted the steps, and knocked on the door. He heard footsteps, and the door swung open. It was Carol.

Avery instinctively removed his hat, and nodded stiffly. "Howdy, ma'am," he said.

"Hello, Mr. Carson, come on in. I just put on a fresh pot of coffee."

"Thank you. Is your father in?"

"He's in his office, but I'll call him." Carol looked over her shoulder toward the kitchen and then turned back to Avery and forced a smile. "Mr. Carson," she said, "I heard about your engagement to Emily Harper. I want to offer my congratulations."

"Thank you, ma'am," Avery said, still standing in the doorway. He wanted to say more but was at a loss for words.

"Carol. Aren't you going to invite Mr. Carson in?" It was Carol's mother calling from the kitchen.

"Ma'am," Avery said. Carol looked at him and he continued. "I'm sorry if I put you in an awkward situation."

Carol's face looked troubled, and then she said, "Mr. Carson, had I known things were so far along with you and Emily, I would never have been so forward. I feel very stupid."

Carol looked down at the floor as her mother stepped through the door, wiping her hands on a dishtowel. "Mr. Carson, come on in. Have you eaten?"

"Yes, ma'am, and thank you."

"Congratulations on your engagement," she said with a sincere smile. "I had a chance to visit with Emily at the dance, and I very much enjoyed her company."

"Thank you. I'll pass on the congratulations."

Mrs. Ball smiled and headed back into the kitchen.

"Miss Ball," Avery said as Carol made to follow her

mother, "please don't feel stupid. I'm honored that you thought me worthy of your affection, and if it weren't for the fact that I'm in love with Emily, I'm sure I'd of been beatin' a trail from my place to here. Emily considers you her best friend."

"Thank you, Mr. Carson. I must admit I'm a little reluctant to face her after I was so obvious."

"Please don't be. Emily needs good friends."

"That's part of the problem," Carol said. "I didn't behave like a good friend. I could tell she liked you, and I wanted to give you something to think about before she had you to herself on the ride home."

Avery was surprised by Carol's candid honesty, but before he could respond, he heard heavy footsteps, and Albert Ball stepped through the door from the living room.

He stopped in midstride and looked at Avery, surprise in his eyes. "Mr. Carson, I didn't hear you come in."

"I only just arrived."

"Congratulations on your engagement."

"Thank you."

Carol left for the kitchen as Ball asked, "What can I do for you?"

Before Avery could answer, Mrs. Ball appeared again in the doorway. "Albert, Mr. Carson, coffee's on the table."

They took their seats, and Ball looked at Avery expectantly.

"Albert," Avery said, "I was just wonderin' where you got your piano."

A look of surprise washed across Ball's face, and it was obvious that the question had caught him off guard. "Why do you ask?" he said.

"I'd like to buy one for Emily for a weddin' present."

"Does she play?" Mrs. Ball asked.

"She did when she was a little girl," Avery replied. "She might want some lessons, I don't know, but she seemed very taken by the fact that you had a piano. I'd like to get her one, but I don't want her to catch wind of it."

"Albert picked this one up when the mines at Medusa failed," Mrs. Ball said. "We had one back in Kansas, and we so missed it."

"I could give Emily lessons if she'd like," Carol interjected.

"I might actually sell you this one," Ball said, looking levelly at Avery, who looked back with interest.

Before Ball could continue, his wife interjected, "It's not a real good piano. The mice had chewed felt off some of the hammers before we got it, so that's why we are getting a new one."

Ball glared at his wife, but the look went unnoticed.

"A couple of the keys stick," she went on, "but they're real low ones that you hardly ever use. I'm sure Emily will like it. My father was a piano tuner, and I'm not bad at it myself, so I could tune it for you after the move."

"That would be great, ma'am," Avery said. Then turning to Ball he asked, "What do you want for it?"

Ball smiled and shook his head. "I'll have to ask the boss," he said.

ᔥ ᔥ

An hour later, Avery was on his way to Bow City. He'd bought the piano, and Ball had agreed to help haul it up through the gap on Avery's return journey. He would bring along a block and tackle and a couple of men to help widen the trail if need be. Avery remembered an underlined verse he'd read from the Bible the night before, about every good thing being a gift from God.

"Thank you," he said out loud. "I know I don't deserve it, but thank you."

He rode into town by midafternoon, and instead of going to the barn, he dismounted in front of the hotel. Emily saw him as he entered the restaurant, and she flashed him a radiant smile. He took his usual seat as she came over with the coffee pot.

"Howdy, beautiful," Avery said. "You're wearin' your Sunday dress."

"That's because I have a new Sunday dress now. Oh, Avery, it's so good to see you. This week seemed like a month."

"It's good to see you too. I reckon I sweated up my horse a bit gettin' here."

Emily looked at him, her eyes full of excitement. "I was supposed to work this evening," she said, "but Miriam's letting me off. I'll be done in half an hour. It's supper at my house tonight."

"That sounds great! I got a few errands to run, and then I'll be right over. You ain't worried about what your nosy neighbor thinks?"

Emily's face broke into a smile. "Not the slightest bit," she said.

武 武

When Avery finished his coffee, he signed the register at the desk and then went to the barn to off saddle. After a brief visit with Wally, he headed for the mercantile. McFadden met him at the counter, and Avery was shocked at his appearance. His nose was swollen, and his eyes looked out from a purple mask that faded to a sickly yellow around his cheeks. Avery made no comment, and though McFadden was obviously uncomfortable, he said nothing.

"Howdy, McFadden," Avery said a little stiffly. "I'd like to open a charge account."

"All right." McFadden reached under the counter and produced a dog-eared ledger, which he placed before him. "Just fill this in here and sign there. The balance is due at the end of every month unless other arrangements are made."

"I want Mrs. Harper to be able to charge things on this account as well," Avery said, watching McFadden to see his reaction.

McFadden looked as if he were going to say something but then changed his mind. "Sure, sure," was all he said.

Avery heard footsteps and turned to see little Timmy McFadden coming up behind him. He was about to look away when he turned and looked again. Timmy McFadden had a black eye. Avery swung his attention back to Timmy's father. Their eyes met, but again nothing was said. He signed the ledger and then reached to shake McFadden's hand. "Thanks, McFadden," he said. "I look forward to doing business with you."

McFadden nodded and then said, "Oh, I almost forgot. I got a letter here for you."

Avery looked up with interest as McFadden went to the wooden cubbyholes on the back wall to retrieve an envelope.

The letter was from Willy Paulson. Avery stepped outside and, standing under the awning in front of the store, ripped open the envelope and read the letter.

To my good friend Avery Carson,

It was good to hear from you and to know that you are well. As per your request, we will start a herd north in the spring. I do, however, have a suggestion for you to consider. I propose that we form the Carson Paulson cattle company. We will only send your younger cows north, and I will add an equal number of my better heifers to the drive. I will look after things here in Texas, and you can manage the northern operation.

As we will want to make an effort to grow the northern herd, there will be a period of time when cash flow will be minimal. Having the established southern end of the operation will provide financial stability to help ensure the northern operation is a success. I am anxious to see the country you described and will come north with the herd in the spring. If you are in agreement, we can finalize the forming of the company at that time.

As per the CP brand, there was one registered in the Galveston area. The brand was owned by the Wellington family, who were heavily involved in the shipping industry. All of their assets were sold about fifteen years ago, and it is believed the only surviving member of the family moved to England from where they originated. The brand has been inactive since that time. I took the liberty to register it in our name, as coincidently, it seemed the obvious choice for the Carson Paulson cattle company.

Your friend,
William Paulson

With a look of satisfaction on his face, Avery folded up the letter and stuffed it in his hip pocket. He stepped down onto the street and headed for the Harper house.

CHAPTER SIXTEEN

Peter was sitting on the front step whittling on a willow stick when Avery approached the house. He stood up and ran to the front gate, and Avery noticed that his hair was neatly combed.

"Hi, Mr. Carson!" he said. "Ma's makin' a fancy supper, and I'm not supposed to get dirty."

Avery chuckled and asked, "Reckon I'm clean enough to pass inspection?"

"Probably," Peter said shrugging his shoulders. "Anyway, grown-ups only gotta wash up when they want to."

Avery smiled. "Let's see that knife of yours," he said. "Is it still holdin' an edge?" Peter handed the knife to Avery, and he felt the blade. "It's not too bad," he said. "I reckon I could touch it up a little though."

"Mr. Carson?"

Avery looked at Peter.

"I'm sure glad you're gonna be my pa."

Avery put a hand on the boy's shoulder and said, "I'm real glad about that too, Peter."

"Ma's sure happy. She walks around the house singing all the time. She never used to do that."

Avery took his hand from Peter's shoulder and said, "Let's go in and see how she's doin'." He led the way up to the house, gave a light knock on the door and then stepped into the kitchen. Emily was at the counter peeling potatoes. She was wearing an apron over her blue dress, with her sleeves rolled up and her hair tied back. She turned and smiled as they entered, and Avery walked over, squeezed her arm, and planted a quick kiss on her lips. Peter stood back watching shyly with big eyes and a smile on his face.

"Boy does it smell good in here!" Avery said.

"Miriam let me sneak out to start the stove and put the roast on," Emily said. "The oven was still warm when I got home, so supper should be ready in about half an hour."

"That's the best news I heard all day," Avery said. "Say, you wouldn't have a stone I could use to put an edge on Peter's knife. I could sharpen up some of your other knives while I'm at it."

"Sorry, I don't have one, but my knives sure could use a sharpening."

"How's about Peter and me run up to the store and get one then," Avery said. "That way I'll have a sharp knife for carvin' up that roast. Oh, and by the way, I set up an account with McFadden at the store, so if you need anythin', you can just charge it."

Emily looked at Avery with a serious but grateful expression. "You're too good to me, Avery," she said softly.

"Ma'am, I couldn't possibly be good enough, and that's a fact."

"I just can't believe how things can change. I'm happier than I dreamed it was possible to be."

Avery smiled at her and said, "We won't be long." Then turning to Peter he said, "Come on, young fella. Let's go buy us a stone."

On the way over to the store, Avery looked at Peter and said, "I couldn't help but notice young Timmy had himself a pretty good shiner."

"Yes, sir," Peter said. "He called Ma that word again, so I did what you said."

Avery thought a moment before saying anything. "You figure Timmy learned anythin'?" he asked.

"I don't know. I don't think he'll call Ma that word anymore."

"I hope not. Just don't stay mad at him, okay? First chance you get, treat him like nothin' happened."

"Yes, sir."

They walked into the mercantile, and the first person they saw was Timmy McFadden. He eyed them warily, and then Peter said, "Hi, Timmy. Mr. Carson is gonna buy a stone so he can sharpen my knife. I'll bet he'll sharpen yours too."

"You got a knife, son?"

"Yes, sir," Timmy said.

"Want me to put an edge on it for you?"

"Sure. It doesn't cut very good anymore."

The boys followed Avery to the counter, where Mabel McFadden was waiting. "Hello, Texas," she said. "I hear you're getting married."

"Yes, ma'am."

"Glad to hear it." Then looking at Peter, she said seriously, "Timmy told me how he got that pretty black eye, and let me tell you, I hurt his bottom worse than you hurt his face." Looking back to Avery, she said, "Mr. Carson, we appreciate your business."

Avery went outside and sat with the boys on the plank walk while he sharpened their knives. When he was finished he said, "We'd best hurry on back, Peter, before your ma throws out the food."

On the walk home, Avery noticed the air had cooled off more than usual, and he wondered if the mild weather had finally run its course. Ahead, they saw a homey light in the window, and when they stepped through the door, the smell of roast beef was almost overpowering. Emily was nowhere to be seen, and she called from the bedroom, "The roast is in the warming oven. I'll be out in a couple of minutes."

Avery found a carving knife in the drawer by the sink, gave it a once over with the new stone, and then set the roast on the counter and began slicing it. He heard Emily enter the room, and when he turned to look at her, his breath caught. Emily had stopped in the doorway, and she smiled at him apprehensively.

She was wearing her new dress, and the silky green material followed the contours of her waist and hips before giving way to a full, gathered skirt that hung in rich folds to the floor. The sleeves were short, revealing her willowy white arms, and the neckline dipped down in a shallow but wide V from her shoulders to about four inches below her throat. She'd piled her hair on top of her head in a loose bun, and it seemed to accentuate her long, graceful neck.

"Wow," Avery said.

"Do you like it?" Emily asked.

"Ma'am, you are absolutely beautiful. Don't move." Avery quickly washed his hands in the sink and dried them on a dish towel. "Peter," he said, "if you don't like to see your ma gettin' kissed, you better close your eyes." He crossed the room to where Emily obediently waited and stood before her a moment before taking her in his arms and kissing her gently on the mouth. He pulled back and then touched her cheek with his hand and said quietly, "What a lovely lady you are. How'd I ever get so lucky?"

Emily kissed him lightly and then looked up at him, her eyes soft and shining. "It's me who's lucky. Thank you for everything, Avery."

Avery shook his head in wonder and then swallowed and said, "We better eat, ma'am." Turning, he looked back at Peter, who hadn't closed his eyes. "Don't worry, son," he said. "You'll get used to it."

෨෨   ෨෨

Avery was up well before sunrise on Monday morning after spending an enjoyable weekend with Emily and

Peter. He'd read them the letter from Willy Paulson, and Emily had seemed pleased, but was surprisingly quiet. When he'd asked her about it, she'd said she was humbled by how many blessings God had heaped upon her. She'd said that going from a social outcast to being the wife of a respected man of means in the community was a little overwhelming and still hard for her to believe.

The ground in the corral behind the barn was frozen hard, and Avery had to break through a layer of ice on the trough before his horse could drink. He saddled up and rode down the street to Emily's, as she had coffee and breakfast waiting. Peter was still asleep, and they enjoyed a quiet time together before he headed out. He'd told Emily that he needed to finish the addition before the snows came, so he wasn't sure when he'd be back. Though Emily didn't protest, he saw the disappointment in her eyes, and he felt a touch of doubt. He hoped he wasn't making the same mistakes all over again, but then he reasoned that the work had to be done, so like it or not, he'd need to get at it. It was a drawn out, reluctant good-bye.

Avery took the trail out of Bow City at a brisk trot, with a timid sun behind him making long shadows on the frosty ground. By the time he sighted the Double Diamond buildings, however, he could feel warmth on his shoulders, and a blue sky overhead was making promises he hoped it could deliver. He rode into the yard and was surprised to see that Ball already had the piano loaded in the back of a wagon and the team hitched up and ready to go. As he was dismounting, he heard the door open up at the house, and turned to see Ball coming down the steps toward him.

"Mornin', Carson," he said as he stepped down off the footbridge.

"It's a frosty one," Avery commented

Ball chuckled and said, "I guess it is where you come from. Better get used to it. It'll soon be gettin' a whole lot colder."

Ball climbed up onto the wagon seat, as the door of the bunkhouse opened and two riders stepped out to mount their waiting ponies. Avery swung up onto his buckskin as they approached.

"Carson, this here's Doc Higgins," Ball said, gesturing toward the wiry old hand Avery had met on his last visit. "You've already met Colby Armstead."

Avery acknowledged their greetings with a nod, and then all three riders fell in behind the wagon as it pulled out.

Armstead pulled up beside him and said, "That was some shindig the other night, wasn't it?"

"Sure was," Avery agreed.

"That's why I like workin' here. Pretty girls to look at every day, an' two dances a year."

"Two dances?"

"Yes, sir. There's a party every spring too, just before we move the cows up to the high country. Ball calls it the 'Last Calf Dance.' Yes, sir, this here's a great outfit to work for."

"Funny, I didn't realize you was workin' for this outfit," Higgins said, speaking for the first time. "What is it you do besides makin' sure your mattress don't blow away?"

"Ha! Don't mind him, Carson," Armstead said. "The sour old pickle ain't happy unless he's miserable. He shoulda been pensioned off years ago 'cept for the fact that the Ball women got a soft spot for kittens, dogs, swayback ponies, an' useless old critters."

Avery smiled. Ahead of him, the piano swayed back and forth in the wagon as Ball picked his way up the slope, changing course every now and then in search of the smoothest terrain. Looking off to the south, Avery saw a long, grassy draw with cattle scattered along either side.

"How's your fall roundup goin'?" he asked Higgins, who was ridding closest to him.

"We're still short a good seventy head. There's plenty of grass up high, and they're comin' in as fat as ticks. The snow'll bring them down eventually I reckon."

"They winter fine on this grass I hear."

"Yep. This grass has a lotta kick. Last winter, we had the most snow I ever saw, and spring was slow comin'. The cattle were a little ribby by the time the grass turned green, but they calved good an' bred back good too."

They'd traveled for a couple of hours when Ball pulled the wagon to a stop, and in spite of the coolness of the day, the team had a sweat on and were breathing hard.

Ball turned in the wagon seat and said, "Why don't you boys grab the shovels and pick from the wagon and ride on ahead. You can scout out the best route and move any rocks and deadfall out of the way."

The closer they got to the gap, the slower their progress became. When they reached the narrowest point above the river, Ball climbed down from the wagon, and the four of them spent a good two hours chipping away at the rock on the uphill side of the trail. Whatever Higgins had said about Armstead being afraid of work proved to be untrue, and Avery was impressed with how much dirt the little man was able to move.

"I figure that should about do it," Ball said, straightening his back and wiping sweat from his forehead.

"I can't tell you how much I appreciate this," Avery told him. "It's provin' to be a bigger job than what I figured."

Ball was still breathing hard. He waved a hand and said, "It ain't nothin'." He paused a moment and then continued. "I was wrong about you, Carson. I'm glad to have you for a neighbor, even if you did break my daughter's heart."

Avery turned his head quickly to look at Ball and then looked away. "You noticed that, did you?" he said.

Ball nodded. "I notice a lotta things where my family's concerned. I may have a thick skull, but I ain't stupid."

"Well if it makes any difference, I can tell you I never done it on purpose."

"I know. For the most part, things have always sorta fallen into place for Carol. She's got to learn some lessons just like the rest of us." They turned and walked back to the wagon. As Avery was throwing his shovel into the box, Ball asked, "You got another way in and out of here?"

"Not that I know of," Avery said. "Why do you ask?"

Ball pointed to a cut in the rock above them. "Looks to me like the river's made it up that high a time or two. I'd be careful usin' this trail in spring runoff. Flash floods are a scary thing."

Avery nodded. "I reckon we'll get snowed in now and then too," he said.

The rest of the trip proved less difficult, and as they pulled into the yard, Ball looked around appreciatively. "I think you'll do fine here," he told Avery. "It might be lonely sometimes though."

Avery nodded. "I hope Emily likes it. I reckon we'll be droppin' in on you from time to time."

Before they unloaded the piano, Avery showed them the foundation he'd laid and the logs he'd been squaring.

"You've done a sight of work here," Ball said. "Had you used a broadax before?"

Avery smiled and said, "No, as a matter of fact. Does it show that bad?"

"No, I reckon your doin' a fair job. I'll bet its slow goin' though."

"I'm gettin' less slow," Avery said, "but it's a chore all right."

Ball nodded then said, "Higgins here's pretty handy with buildin'. He did most of the log work on my house and barn. Why don't I leave him here for a few days to give you a hand? The two of you'll have this up in no time."

Avery looked at Ball and said appreciatively, "That's right neighborly of you Ball. Trouble is, I think I'm windin' up on the wrong side of a big debt."

Ball shrugged it off. "Things tend to even out over time," he said.

Avery went into the house, started the fire, and put the coffee on, while Ball backed the wagon up to the door and his men took the lash ropes off the piano. It was a chore getting it off the wagon and through the door, but when it was in place against the east wall between the two leather chairs, Avery felt a deep sense of satisfaction.

Ball wanted to get home before dark, so though everyone was hungry, Avery didn't take the time to cook anything. Instead, they all had cold pan bread with their coffee, and a short time later, Avery and Higgins stood watching as the wagon rolled away back to the gap.

GHAPTER SEVENTEEN

iggins's help proved to be invaluable. The two men got an early start the next day, and before the morning was through, they had the beams for the floor set into the foundation. In the afternoon, Higgins worked at squaring more timbers while Avery used some of the planks in the barn to cover the floor. By the following morning, they were laying logs.

Because the addition would settle, they spiked vertical logs about four inches apart where the walls would butt up against the cabin. The logs on the addition were notched to fit into these sleeves so that, as they shrunk, the joint would stay tight. Higgins showed Avery how to make a dovetail joint on the two outer corners, and by the afternoon of the third day, he was laying logs while Higgins squared up the remaining timbers.

Three days later, when Higgins headed back to the Double Diamond, the ridgepole and rafters rested on sturdy walls, and all that was left for Avery to do was close in the roof and the gable end. Two days after that, with the addition all but complete, he saddled up and took the trail to Bow City. He took along his packhorse, as he hoped to bring back some mortar for chinking and glass for a window.

The weather had changed during the night, and he rode out under a heavy, gray sky that shrouded the mountains to well below the timberline. He wondered at the wisdom of making the trip, but he was anxious to see Emily and Peter, so he pressed on. About a mile out of Bow City, small hard flakes of snow driven by a gusty north wind began to rattle off his hat, and he turned up his collar and tucked his chin to his chest.

The town's main street was surprisingly active, and as he dismounted in front of the barn, he noted that several horses stood hunkered down in front of the hotel. *Emily will be busy*, he thought, feeling a sense of disappointment. He'd hoped she'd have had time for a break and a visit, but it looked as if they were out of luck. He off saddled and left his horses in the barn and then crossed the street to the restaurant.

The room was crowded, and Emily, wearing one of her gray dresses, was pouring coffee at the back table. She saw him, and there was surprise in her smile.

Someone spoke off to his right. "Howdy, Avery. Sit down an' take a load off." It was Wally, and he was seated at the table closest to the door. "I seen you ride in, but I figured you'd rather have me save you a spot then come an' watch you unsaddle."

"Thanks," Avery said. He unbuttoned his coat before

sitting down as Emily wound her way through the crowd, coming over to their table.

"Hello, Avery," she said, her voice showing her pleasure. "I'm so glad to see you."

"I'm mighty glad to see you too, Emily. You couldn't do somethin' to get yourself fired could you? I'd like to sneak you out of here."

Emily giggled. "We're not so lucky as last time you were in town," she said. "This is the busiest I've ever seen it in here."

"Well just be real slow about pourin' that coffee so I can talk to you as well as look at you."

"Oh, Avery, I've been watching that door every day hoping it would be you that came through. When I saw the snow start to fall, I about gave up on today."

"Tell you what," Avery said. "How's about when I'm done with my coffee, I go and pick up Peter. I'll get him somethin' to eat, and then at least the three of us can be in the same room together."

"That sounds good," Emily said smiling. "I better run. Maybe things will slow down later."

The hot coffee tasted good and it, along with the warmth in the room, slowly took the chill from Avery's bones. He enjoyed the busy hum of conversation and the small talk with Wally and the other men at his table. Emily stopped by and topped up their cups, and when he'd finished, he dismissed himself and left to get Peter.

It had stopped snowing, but a light skiff swirled along the street and the wind was raw where it found its way between the buildings. Peter was excited to see him, and as they headed for the restaurant, Avery noticed that his arms were a little long for his threadbare coat.

"Is that the jacket you wear for cold weather?" he asked.

"Yes, sir. When it gets really cold, I wear a wool sweater underneath it."

"Well it looks to me like you've been doin' some growin' and the jacket ain't keepin' up. What's say we stop by the mercantile and see if they got any jackets for a fella your size?"

Peter looked up at him with serious eyes. "Should I ask Ma first?" he said. "She says we shouldn't impose on your hostility."

Avery chuckled. "I'm sure she'll be fine with it."

Avery ended up buying Peter a new wool coat, some one-piece long johns, and a new pair of overalls.

When they entered the restaurant, it was still busy. Wally had left, and they took a seat at the long table in the center of the room. They only had time for brief snatches of conversation with Emily, and Peter was eager to tell her about his new clothes. When they'd eaten, Avery took Peter home, and after spending some time making a slingshot, he helped him get ready for bed. After tucking him in, he sat on the foot of Peter's bed while he said his prayers.

When Avery stood to leave, Peter said, "Mr. Carson."

Avery turned to look at him.

"When we move out to the ranch, will you teach me how to be a cowboy?"

"You bet, Peter. I'll get you ridin' a horse so you can help me look after the cattle."

"That'll be fun. Good night."

"Good night."

Avery went to the kitchen, stoked the fire and then put a pot of coffee on and settled down to wait. It wasn't long before he heard footsteps outside, and he rose to meet Emily coming through the door. Her cheeks were rosy, and she had snowflakes in her hair. He didn't wait for her to take her coat off but took her in his arms and kissed her passionately. Her cheeks were cold and fresh on his, but her lips were soft and warm, and when he pulled back from her, her eyes shone in the lamplight.

"I can't wait to be married," she said. "I wish you didn't have to leave."

"Me too. I'll stay for a while if you're not too tired."

"I'm tired, but I don't care. I could stay up all night. Is Peter sleeping?"

Avery nodded. "I ain't never tucked a kid into bed before. I kinda like it."

Emily smiled as she removed her coat. "I can't tell you how much it means to me that you and Peter get along so well. You're his hero, Avery."

"I'm sure more time with me will cure that. I really want to do a good job of bein' his pa though. 'Course I've never been one before, but I guess it's a learn-as-you-go sorta thing."

Emily smiled and put her arms around Avery's waist and her face against his chest. He held her close and cupped the back of her head in his hand.

"I smell coffee boilin'," he said.

"I've got some cake in the pantry."

They sat together at the kitchen table and talked well into the night. Avery didn't leave for the hotel till two in the morning, leaving tracks in the new snow that blanketed the ground.

∽   ∽

The first thing Avery did when he woke the next morning was look out his hotel window. For obvious reasons, getting snowed in at Bow City had its appeal, but he was anxious to get back to the ranch and get everything ready for Emily and Peter to move in. The snow had let up during the night, but the sky looked threatening, so he decided it would be best to make an early start. Because he'd kept Emily up so late the night before, he figured he'd get his horses and see about buying glass and mortar before going to see her. After paying for his room, he crossed the street to the barn. He was surprised to see Wally was already hard at work cleaning stalls.

"Mornin', Wally," he said as he approached.

Wally threw a forkful of manure into a wheelbarrow and then straightened up. Leaning on his fork, he asked, "You headin' back up country?"

"Soon I reckon."

"My bad knee tells me there's more snow comin', and it don't usually lie."

"Hopefully I don't get snowed in up there," Avery said thoughtfully. "I got a weddin' to get to."

"No tellin' what the weather'll do," Wally said. "We had more snow last year than other winters, but it never kept the Double Diamond from makin' it to town. If you can make it through the gap, you should be all right."

As Avery threw his saddle on his buckskin he asked, "Wally, you wouldn't know anyone who's got a dead broke horse for sale? I'm lookin' for somethin' Peter'll be able to ride."

"Not off hand I don't. I'll keep my eyes open for you, though."

"Thanks, I'd appreciate it. Don't say nothin' to Peter about it though. I want it to be a surprise."

Wally nodded. "I guess Christmas is comin'," he said.

Avery smiled his good-bye and then led his horses the short distance to the mercantile. He was glad to find it open and purchased two sheets of glass packed in light wooden crates and two sacks of mortar. He fastened one sack and one piece of glass on each side of the sawbuck with a box hitch and then threw on a diamond with the lash cinch. After double checking the load, he mounted up and rode over to Emily's. She met him at the door.

"I see you're packed and ready to go," she said.

Avery nodded. "I'd like to stay longer," he said, "but I want to get back before the snow's too deep, as I got a few more things to do to get the house ready."

Avery stepped inside and closed the door quickly to shut out the cold. He smelled coffee and bacon and saw that the table was set on a silky green table cloth. Emily noticed him looking at it, and said, "I hope you don't mind.

I had quite a bit of material left, and it seemed a shame to waste it. I could have almost sewn two dresses."

Avery chuckled. "I had no idea how much cloth to buy," he said. "Mrs. McFadden sold me enough for a woman her size, and I wasn't about to argue."

Emily smiled and then said, "I'll go wake Peter. He won't want to miss you."

∽ ∽

The breeze was out of the northeast, so it was at Avery's back on the trip home. Snow sifted across the trail and the flat, dull light painted the landscape with the same brush as it did the sky. His horses were eager to travel, and with his collar turned to the wind, he made good time.

As he drew abreast the Double Diamond, he hesitated and then turned up the laneway. Higgins and another hand were pitching hay to some horses in the corral, and his packhorse eyeing the feed, nickered eagerly.

"Howdy, Carson," Higgins called as he approached. "I seen you ride by yesterday, so I figured you must of got the roof closed in."

"I did," Avery said, "just in time to beat the snow too."

"Stoppin' in to warm up a bit?" Higgins asked.

"I ain't that cold really," Avery replied. "It's not too bad with the wind at your back. I'm lookin' to buy young Peter a horse, and I need somethin' dead broke. I was ridin' by and got to thinkin' maybe Ball had an old hay burner around that wasn't earnin' its keep."

"I'd say he's got two or three right here. Them girls get mighty sentimental about the critters around here, so there's a few ain't nothin' but pets."

Avery quickly scanned the horses in the corral and noted that they were all either long in the tooth or one and two year olds.

"If he'd let him go, I'd take that Appaloosa there," Higgins said, gesturing with his thumb toward a big, rawboned horse with wide feet and a long sad looking face.

"He ain't much to look at, but he's sound as a dollar, honest as the day is long, and he's got a heart of gold. Carol's been ridin' him since she was about six."

Avery looked at Higgins and said, "That must make him real old."

"He is that. No one around here knows his age for sure, but like I say, he's sound. If he can get you through the next couple or three years, the boy will be ready for somethin' a little more salty anyway. Here, I'll grab a halter from the barn and you can take him for a little ride."

Avery climbed into the corral for a closer look while Higgins left for the barn. The Appy wasn't the horse he'd of chosen on looks alone, but looks weren't everything, and the horse had a good, kind eye. Higgins came back with the halter, and Avery swung up and went for a short ride around the pasture. The old horse handled like a dream, and before he swung back to the barn, he knew he could do no better. He dismounted in the corral and stripped off the halter.

"What do ya think?" Higgins asked.

"That's the horse I want all right. Now, I just hope Ball will sell him."

"Let's head up to the house and find out."

Avery had to make his deal with Carol, and in the end he bought not only the horse but a small saddle she'd grown out of. He could tell she was torn between having to let the horse go and wanting Peter to have him. She followed Avery to the barn, and after a tearful farewell and several hugs around the horse's neck, she was willing to let him go.

"You got a name for this pony?" Avery asked.

"His name is Willy, and please don't change it."

"Willy it is. You can come an' visit him anytime. If you arm wrestle Peter for it, he might even let you ride him."

∞ ∞

Avery tied Willy and his packhorse head-to-tail, mounted up, and headed for the gap. He'd been riding for about an hour when the snow began to fall, and soon it was like a heavy curtain that shut out the light. By the time he reached the pass, his horses were slugging through a foot of snow, and the raging river, just a stone's throw to his right, was lost from sight.

He felt his horses' gait quicken before he saw the outline of his buildings, and then a horse whinnied ahead of him. Avery cautiously reined in as he saw four gray shapes of mounted men materialize out of the gloom.

He unbuttoned his coat and tucked it behind his pistol, pulled off his right glove, and blew into his hand. Then he moved slowly forward. One of the riders came toward him, and the first thing Avery noticed was that he was an Indian, and then he recognized him as the man who had returned his packhorse. Both men pulled up, and the Indian raised a hand, palm forward.

Avery did the same.

"We have good hunt," the Indian said. "Bring meat."

Avery nodded, unsure of what was happening.

"You bring meat. Feed squaw. Feed papoose in big snow. We bring meat now."

Avery wondered at the comment, and then realized they mistook him for Clancy, and that Clancy must have helped them during the last winter. It struck him as odd, for it meant that he must bear a striking resemblance to the man he'd buried, and it maybe explained why they'd returned his horse. He realized too, that Clancy's kindness had probably saved his life.

"Thank you," he said. "Meat is good." He rubbed his belly, and the Indian smiled and nodded.

Avery sat his horse facing the Indians, and they sat facing him. No one moved, and he was unsure what to do. He was cold and anxious to get inside, so he smiled, nodded his head, and rode past them into the yard.

The Indians fell silently in behind.

As Avery dismounted and began to off saddle, he was alarmed that the Indians began to do the same. He looked at the sky and the fading light and realized they must be planning to spend the night. He was uncomfortable

197

with the idea but figured he had no choice in the matter. Glancing over at the Indians, he noticed the man who'd ridden off with his saddle was in the group, and he still had the saddle. Avery smiled and shook his head.

One of the men walked toward him, carrying two hind quarters of venison. He looked questioningly at Avery, and Avery motioned for him to follow. He went to the storage shed, felt around in the dark, and found a rope. While the Indian watched, blocking what little light came through the door, Avery hung the meat from an overhead beam. Turning he smiled at the man and rubbed his belly again. Again it brought the same response.

Avery threw his gear in the barn, and the others followed suit. When he turned his horses loose in the horse pasture, they did the same. When he walked to the cabin, they followed him in silent, single file.

Once inside, Avery lit a couple of lamps and started a fire in the stove. It was cold in the room, so he kept his coat on. The Indian men did the same and took seats on the floor, watching his every move. They couldn't hide their curiosity when he pulled aside the bearskin rug and lifted the trapdoor to the cellar. When he came back up with a slab of bacon and some flour, the man who'd brought him the venison smiled and rubbed his belly. All the other men chuckled, and Avery found himself laughing with them.

He cooked up the bacon, made some pan bread, and opened a couple of tins of beans. He wasn't sure if his guests would drink it, but he also made a large pot of coffee. The cabin began to warm up, and when the meal was ready, he joined them on the floor, and they ate in silence. Next he served the coffee, and whether or not they'd had it before, he couldn't tell. They watched him, and when he slowly began sipping the hot drink, they did the same.

Finally, the Indian who seemed to be the leader spoke. "Food good. No need squaw."

Apparently the others understood because this brought a chuckle.

"I have a squaw," Avery said. "She is coming soon. Papoose coming soon."

The Indian nodded and, with a questioning look, made a gesture with his hands in front of his belly. Avery realized he was asking if his squaw was pregnant. He shook his head no and made a motion with his hand to show how high Peter was from the floor.

"Papoose," he said, and the Indian nodded. On an impulse, Avery stood and walked over to the piano. Turning to face the men on the floor he said, "Gift for squaw."

He then tinkled some of the keys, and the surprised looks on their faces made him chuckle. He played a few more notes and then motioned with his hands for them to try.

They looked from one to another, and then the man who'd carried the venison stood up. He walked over to the piano, hesitated, and then banged twice on the keys. He jumped back, and his face lit up. Then he looked quickly over his shoulder at the other men and hit the keys again. Soon all the men were around the piano taking their turns. This kept them entertained for quite some time, and then, one by one, they took their seats on floor.

One of the men lay down, and Avery figured they were getting ready to sleep, so he said good night, added wood to the fire, and then carried one of the lamps to his room. He drew his pistol and put it under his pillow and then kicked off his boots and climbed into bed with his clothes on. He blew out the light and lay staring at the ceiling, wondering if he could sleep. A few tentative notes sounded on the piano, and someone laughed. Not long after that, Avery slept.

He came awake with the dim gray light of dawn filtering through a frosted window. He heard movement from the other room and then the sound of the door closing softly. Throwing back the covers, he swung his feet to the floor, reached under his pillow for his pistol, and returned it to his holster. No one was in the cabin, but he heard voices outside. He threw some sticks on the coals in the firebox and coaxed them into flames. When he felt sure they'd caught, he pulled on his coat and hat and stepped outside.

The Indians had their horses, and a couple of them were mounted. Seeing Avery, the man who'd done the speaking walked over.

"Ride one day," he said, pointing south. "Follow small river of stones where sun go down." Motioning west, he continued, "Plenty wood. Plenty grass. Plenty good hunt. You come."

Avery nodded. "Maybe I will," he said.

The Indian put his hand on his chest and said, "Small Bear."

"Avery Carson," Avery said, tapping his own chest.

"Avery Carson," Small Bear repeated slowly.

Suddenly, a thought occurred to Avery. Pointing south he asked, "Have you seen any white men down that way?"

Small Bear looked south, and for a moment, he said nothing. Then turning to Avery he said, "They no come. We no go." He made a throwaway motion with his right hand and said, "Bad place for Shoshoni. Big smoke. Big noise. Plenty bad man."

Avery nodded, his face serious. "Come again, friend," he said.

Small Bear nodded. "Friend," he said. When he'd mounted his horse, the Indians rode out around the barn and headed south without looking back.

CHAPTER EIGHTEEN

Avery spent the morning cutting a hole in the wall and installing the window. He then caught his horse and led him to the barn to saddle up. When he stepped through the door, he stopped short. There on a rail between two stalls, next to the saddle he'd been using, was his old saddle. Avery walked forward in disbelief and then stopped again. Fastened with rawhide to the billet strap was a large hunting knife in an ornately beaded leather sheath. Shaking his head, he bent and admired the workmanship. Then, with a keen sense of anticipation, he pulled the saddle off the rail and threw it on his buckskin. He led the horse outside, mounted up, and turned for the canyon to see how the cattle were fairing. The saddle felt like coming home, and he smiled both with contentment and at the humor of the situation.

It had stopped snowing and the sky was partially clear, but it hadn't warmed up any. The cattle seemed well fed and content, and so, satisfied, Avery rode back down the hill and used the rest of the afternoon to drag in deadfall from the aspen bluff. The following day was spent with a bucksaw replenishing the woodpile.

By late afternoon, a light breeze was blowing out of the southwest, and the temperature began to rise. Overnight, the breeze turned into a strong wind, and by morning, Avery woke to a world of melting snow and running water. On impulse, he saddled up, stuffed his saddlebags with food, and tied on his bedroll. He was about to mount up, but then he dropped his reins and went back into the house. From a drawer by his bed, he grabbed a small roll of bills, which he shoved in his pocket.

He struck south, hoping the weather would hold long enough for him to find his way to the settlement Small Bear had spoken of. He still had hopes of finding information on the man who'd built the cabin, and this could be his last chance before spring.

Throughout the morning, he followed the tracks made by the Indians, moving at an easy mile-eating trot, keeping the river on his right. By midafternoon, the trail became less clear, as much of the snow had melted. He came to a place where the river forked and, by the tracks in the mud, could see that the Indians had forded the main branch and then followed the smaller tributary to the west. Small Bear had said it was a day's ride, but with a couple hours of daylight left, he pressed on south. The river was narrower now and running swiftly as the valley floor began a gradual climb toward a flat-topped, pine-covered ridge.

It forked again, with the right fork tumbling from a steep timber-chocked draw that appeared to be virtually impassable. Avery followed the left fork, and as he entered the trees along the bank, he saw an old scar in the bark of a tree where either eveners or a wheel hub had rubbed against it. Looking ahead, he made out a trail, not by markings on the ground but by a space between the trees large enough for a wagon to pass. With a growing sense of excitement, he moved out at a brisk pace, every now and then noticing more scars on trees or deadfall that had been sawn and removed from the trail. He was making a long, steady climb into heavier timber as the light began to fade.

He slowed his pace, as it was becoming harder to follow the trail, and here and there, deadfall blocked his way. He was suddenly aware that he no longer heard water running, and he realized he must have climbed higher than the headwaters of the river. With little to no grass under the trees, and knowing his horse would be hungry, and not wanting to make a dry camp, he kept moving. He could no longer see the trail, but overhead, a small gap in the trees where he saw the winking of a few stars gave him confidence. It came to him then that if this was, indeed, the trail taken by his predecessor, his horse would have been over it a time or two, so he let him have his head.

Less than an hour later, he broke free of the trees, and as the terrain leveled off, he found himself on a flat, rocky ridge with nothing above him but the star-covered sky. The horse moved willingly forward, and soon they were dropping back into the darkness of the forest. Not long after that, Avery heard running water off to his left, and then they were in a small, grass-covered clearing. The gelding stopped of its own accord, and Avery dismounted stiffly, wondering if the horse's previous owner hadn't camped there before.

※ ※

When he broke camp the next morning, Avery could see he was still well above the valley floor and that not far ahead the timber played out. As far as he could see, the landscape looked cold, harsh, and inhospitable. Across the creek, however, he saw a distinct gap in the trees, and he knew he was still on the trail.

Throughout the day, he followed a tumbling creek that ran between two rocky ridges, barren of grass and broken only by scattered trees, whose stunted and twisted shapes bore testament to a difficult existence. The hard, lifeless ground gave few hints of a trail, but with only one possible direction of travel, Avery continued down the long and steady grade.

As evening was approaching, the valley took a hard turn to the east, and almost at once, he intercepted a trail that was both well-worn and recently used. Ahead, it followed the valley to a widening gap in the hills, but where Avery sat his horse, it cut hard to the southwest, climbing a steep, gravely slope. Nailed to a long-dead stump was a crudely painted sign that read "Jolly Roger Silver Mine." Avery gazed up the slope, and then at an almost impossible height, perched on the face of a cliff, he spotted a crude tarpaper shack.

He continued down the trail and, here and there,

passed signs of abandoned diggings. Other trails branched off to climb the hills in either direction, and then as darkness settled in, he broke out into the open and saw lights spread out below him. Dark peaks, ominous against the night sky hovered over the town, and as Avery descended down the final grade, a shrill piercing whistle shrieked in the darkness, once, twice, and then a third time. Avery had no idea what it meant, but it seemed a foreboding welcome.

He entered the town by a darkened side street and, a few blocks ahead, could see lights and activity. Common sense told him that the stables would be at the east end of town, so he turned left a block before the main street. His guess proved correct, and he was soon dismounting in the deep shadows behind the barn. No one was around, so he tied his horse in an empty stall and, by the dim light of a single coal oil lantern, off saddled and then pitched down some hay from the loft.

When he'd fed his horse, he left to see about a meal for himself and a room for the night. He crossed the street and shouldered his way along a crowded boardwalk, passing three saloons and two gambling houses before reaching a hotel with its adjoining restaurant. His room cost four times what it would in Bow City, but he'd expected as much, and after pocketing his key, he entered the crowded eating area. The air was thick and warm and stank of unwashed bodies and greasy food. Avery spied an empty chair at a table in the middle of the room and worked his way across a mud-caked floor and took a seat. An undernourished waitress, whose haggard face looked as if she'd been working double shifts, wordlessly took his order and then left for the kitchen.

"Third time in four months." The speaker was a broad-shouldered man with close-cropped blond hair and big, calloused hands.

"I tell you, Pridis don't care so long as he's makin' a profit."

"He don't care as long as he's got fools willin' to take the places of them that get killed," a balding man with a course, black beard said.

"What happened?" Avery asked as the waitress returned and deposited his plate in front of him.

"Mine cave-in at the Lucky Lady," the first speaker said angrily. "Seventeen men trapped, and no one knows if they're alive or dead. Six men were buried alive just two weeks ago."

"Was that why the whistle blew a while back?" Avery asked.

"You got it," the man replied. He wiped the leftover grease from his plate with a crust of bread; stuffed it in his mouth; and, still chewing, turned and asked Avery, "So what's a cow nurse like you doin' in Stanfield? Tradin' in your spurs for a double jack?"

Before Avery could answer, the bearded man interjected bitterly, "I reckon there'll be some job openin's at the Lucky Lady."

Avery shook his head and said, "No thanks, I reckon I'd just as soon work where I can see the sky. I'm here to try an' find some information about a man."

"You the law?" the blond man asked.

"No, sir, just a cowman. I'm hopin' to find someone who remembers a gent trailin' some cattle through here a while back. Had some white-faced bulls with 'im."

"They're always trailin' cattle in here," Black Beard said. "Best fella to talk to would be Oscar Johnson. He owns the butcher shop, and he's been here from the beginnin'. Next block west, same side of the street."

Avery nodded his thanks, and when the talk shifted to speculating on plans for the rescue effort and the possible causes for the cave-in, he finished his meal in silence.

He was sure he'd need to wait till morning, but with nothing to lose, he left the restaurant and made his way to the butcher shop. To his surprise, a light showed in the window, and when he tried the door, it opened. A bell hanging from the door frame tinkled as he entered, and a stocky young man wearing a bloody apron came through a door behind the counter.

"Is Oscar Johnson in?" Avery asked.

The young man glanced at Avery's boots and spurs and then looked up and said, "One minute."

He disappeared through the door, and a short time later, an older version of the man stepped out, wiping his hands on a rag. "You've got beef to sell?" he asked.

"No, sir," Avery replied. "I'm lookin' for information about someone you may have met."

The man scowled and asked, "Are you the law?"

"That's the second time I've been asked that tonight," Avery said, pushing his hat back on his head. "No, I ain't the law. I'm just wonderin' if you remember a fella pushin' a few cows and some white-faced bulls through here a while back. They was branded CP on the left hip. Maybe he sold you some beef."

Oscar thought a moment and then said, "Yes, I remember him. Are you his brother?"

Avery felt a surge of hope, and ignoring the question asked, "What do you remember?"

"He came and talked to me. He said he planned on ranching somewhere north of here and wanted to know if I'd be interested in buying beef from him. I wouldn't have remembered except for the bulls you mentioned. Good-looking animals."

"Did you get his name?" Avery asked.

"I'm sure he told me, but I don't remember. I never saw him again, so I figured his ranching venture didn't pan out. Far as I know, there's no grass to speak of north of here."

Avery was visibly disappointed.

"Sorry. I'd help you if I could."

"That's all right. Thanks." Before he turned to go Avery asked, "You reckon anyone else in town would know somethin' about him?"

Oscar shook his head. "I doubt it. He wasn't here long, and Stanfield's population has a fast turnover."

"What about a hardware store? He bought a new stove here I reckon. I'm pretty sure he was in town more than once."

"Could be," Oscar said. "But I think you're out of luck."

Avery looked at him questioningly.

"The hardware store burned down about a year back.

business."

Avery thanked the man and then went back out on the street. Anymore inquiries would have to wait till morning, he reasoned, so he turned and headed for his hotel room. Maybe come daylight he'd track down the sheriff and see if he knew anything.

He was about to enter the hotel when, down the street, he noticed activity in front of the livery stable. By the light that spilled through the doorway, he could see three leggy horses being led inside, and then it came to him. Maybe the hostler at the barn knew something. If the man he'd buried had been in town a time or two, he'd have left his horse at the barn. Maybe he'd rented a wagon there when he'd moved supplies. Avery stepped down off the boardwalk and, with a purposeful stride, took the less crowded street to the barn.

Three men and four horses crowded the dimly lit alleyway. A fourth man was standing in the stall with Avery's buckskin, and assuming it was the hostler, Avery placed a hand on the hindquarter of a big bay and walked around the horse to face him.

"Is this your horse?" the man asked, his face hidden by the shadow of his hat brim.

"Yeah, it's mine," Avery said. "You weren't here when I rode in, so I helped myself."

Avery froze as he heard a pistol being cocked behind him, and then as the man in front of him pushed back his hat, he felt the shock of recognition like a fist being slammed into his chest. He was the tall man Avery had seen on the street in Bow City just before the holdup, the outlaw who had gotten away. The man stepped out from behind Avery's horse, grinning wickedly.

"Well if this ain't the luck of the devil," he said. "The pistol fighter from Bow City and the man that busted up O'Donnell are one in the same. I shoulda guessed it when I seen his little pigeon in the bank there."

Avery stood feet apart, his mind racing. *Busted up O'Donnell? Where had he heard that name?* He glanced at the open door at the back of the barn but knew it was hopeless. Then it hit him. *O'Donnell! Mike O'Donnell! The man Emily had run away from!* Fear and anger rose in his chest, and he felt his body become a tight coiled spring.

"Lift his gun, Billy. I know Mike's gonna want him for himself, but I don't think he'll mind if I mark him up a little."

Avery felt a pistol in his back and then his gun being taken.

"I lost three good men in Bow City. One of them was my brother." The tall man's expression turned ugly as he twisted his mouth and drove a fist at Avery's face with everything he had.

Avery instinctively ducked his head to the side and the blow skidded off his ear. As the outlaw's chest collided with his shoulder, Avery drove his right fist into the man's unprotected stomach. He followed it with a right uppercut to the chin and then hooked a short left over the man's extended right arm. Avery felt himself being grabbed from behind but managed to drive a knee into the tall rider's face as he was going down. The man fell to his hands and

211

knees and then quickly staggered back to his feet, trying to drag air into lungs that refused to cooperate.

Doubled over, he wheezed out bitter curses and then managed to say, "Hold him still." When he could stand upright, he faced Avery, breathing heavily, hot murder in his eyes. "You're gonna find out you ain't so tough, hardcase. I just wish I didn't have to save you for Mike."

As the tall rider slowly and deliberately drew back his fist, Avery lifted his right foot and drove a spur into the shin of one of the men holding him. The man yelled in pain, and with his arms still pinned, Avery dove forward, smashing his forehead into the tall rider's face. The men behind him lost their grip, and Avery fell to his knees among dancing hooves. A heavy weight piled down between his shoulder blades, followed by an explosion of light in his brain and a sharp ringing in his ears that quickly faded to nothing.

∽ ∽

Avery's consciousness crept in slowly like a cold, gray dawn, and with it came the pain. He opened his eyes to darkness—darkness and two thin yellow lines that gradually became one. He was lying face down on a cold, wooden floor, the only light coming from under a door a few feet away. He became aware of voices and piano music coming from somewhere not far off. He tried to move, but a sharp pain in his side caused him to gasp and fall back to the floor, and then he realized his hands were tied behind his back. With great effort he tried to think, to remember. *He'd been in a fight, and it had something to do with the robbery in Bow City. Emily had been in the bank. Emily!*

Piece by piece, it was coming back to him. He tried to move his feet but found they were tied as well. He had no idea what to do and it was hard to concentrate, so for a while, he did nothing. His head throbbed with every beat of his heart, and from the way his ribs felt, he was sure they'd put the boots to him once he'd been down. Slowly as his mind cleared, a stubborn will to fight and win took hold.

They were taking him to Mike O'Donnell, the man who'd beaten Emily, the man who was Peter's father. He was O'Donnell's bitter enemy, and he'd never even met the man. By some fantastic twist of fate, he'd ended up taking the place of Emily's liberator, and by another strange twist, he happened to be the man's lookalike. He remembered Emily's reaction the first time she'd seen his horse.

"You remind me of someone," she'd said.

His horse with the angel wings on its hip had unwittingly betrayed him. No doubt word had gotten back to O'Donnell that the man who'd put Emily on the stage had ridden the horse, and Mike would have been on the lookout ever since. Mike would kill him; this he knew for certain. The outlaw from Bow City had recognized Emily, so no doubt O'Donnell knew where she was. She was in danger, and unless he could somehow escape, she would be utterly helpless. He tried the ropes that held him, but there was no give. He twisted his wrists back and forth, his movements becoming more frantic as frustration set in.

Finally he lay still, his breathing hard. He had to think. He looked around the dark room, hoping to find some sharp metal edge he could rub the ropes against. He saw the black shape of a heavy desk close to his feet and against the back wall; maybe there would be something there. Then he saw the window. He tried worming his way closer, and then in despair, realized his feet were tied to the desk. With a heavy sigh, he collapsed onto his back and lay still. It was hopeless.

Staring at the ceiling, he began to mull over the strange events that had brought him to this place. It was a tumble of thoughts that wandered hit and miss, and then he was remembering words he'd read from the dead man's Bible:

> *This I recall to mind, therefore have I hope. It is of the Lord's mercies that we are not consumed, because His compassions fail not. They are new every morning: great is Thy faithfulness.*

Then some more of what he'd read came to mind:

> *Trust in the Lord with all thine heart; and lean not on thine own understanding. In all thy ways acknowledge Him, and He will direct thy paths.*

All at once he knew for sure. This wasn't just some

strange twist of fate. It was providence. Everything was far too fantastic to credit to chance. He remembered Emily saying she'd prayed that God would send an angel to deliver her and that the man who'd put her on the stage had been that angel. Avery knew he was no angel, but he felt a new courage.

"God help me," he whispered.

He heard footsteps outside the door followed by silence. The doorknob began to turn, and he lay down flat, feigning unconsciousness. The door opened quickly and then was almost instantly closed, and in the brief moment of light, Avery saw that a dance hall girl had entered the room.

"Hey, mister, can you hear me?" she whispered.

"Yes, ma'am," Avery whispered back. He heard her cross the room toward him, feeling her way in the dark. Afraid she'd trip on him, he said softly, "I'm down here on the floor."

She knelt down beside him, and Avery could feel her closeness and smell her strong perfume.

"I got a knife. Lay still an' I'll cut you loose."

"Who are you?" Avery asked.

"A friend of Emily's. You need to ride, mister."

Avery rolled over on his stomach, and the girl felt down his arm to his wrists. He pulled his hands as far apart as he could, hoping she wouldn't mistakenly cut him.

"I heard 'em talkin'," she whispered. "Travis thinks none of us girls got ears. You're the fella that beat up Mike an' then helped Emily an' Peter get away."

"It's a long story," Avery said. He heard and felt her sawing at his ropes, and so far, she hadn't nicked him.

"Well, listen up, mister, an' listen good. Travis done told Mike where Emily's livin', an' he's gone to get her back. He went with one o' his freight outfits up to Cheyenne, an' he's fixin' to swing by an' pick her up on the way back to Denver. Like I said, you gotta ride."

"So O'Donnell owns this place too?" Avery asked.

"Mike owns lot's o' things. He's in love with money and little else. Money and power. I don't think he ever cared a lick for Emily. He just liked stickin' her up where everyone could see her, knowin' every man in camp wanted her, but he had her."

Avery felt the ropes on his wrist loosen. "I think that's good, ma'am," he said.

When the girl quit sawing he began pulling at the ropes, and in a matter of seconds, his hands were free. Wordlessly, she handed him the knife and watched in silence while he began cutting the ropes around his ankles.

"What's gonna happen to you if they figure out you're the one who turned me loose?" Avery asked.

"Oh they'll know it's me," the girl said. "I'm the only one who's on break."

"What'll they do to you?"

"It ain't important. I already thought it all through." She paused and then said softly, "Emily was the best friend I ever had. You take care of her, mister."

"We're gettin' married in a little over a week," Avery said as the ropes on his ankles fell away.

"God bless you."

Avery ignored the pain and struggled to his feet. He was instantly dizzy and stumbled forward to grab the edge of the desk.

"You okay?" the girl asked.

"I'll be fine; just give me a minute. Do you know where they put my gun and my hat?" he asked.

"I don't know about your hat, but your pistol's in the room next door. Trouble is, so is Travis an' his three gunnies."

"I'll need a gun," Avery said.

After a moment of silence, the girl said, "I'll be right back."

She slipped out the door, and Avery was left to wait in the dark. A burst of raucous laughter erupted through the thin wall, and then the piano began pounding out another tune. Avery practiced walking from the desk to the door and then back again.

He turned when he heard the door open and saw the dance hall girl slide through, and then they were in darkness. She came close and slid a cold pistol into Avery's hand.

"It's the best I could do," she whispered.

Avery could tell from the feel that it was an old Navy cap and ball, and he asked, "Is it loaded?"

"Yes."

"What's your name, ma'am?"

"Holly Metcalf," she said. "Say hello to Emily an' Peter for me. How is little Peter?"

"He's a fine boy, ma'am." Avery paused and then asked

unexpectedly, "What about you? What was you like as a little girl?"

Holly was taken aback by the question, and after a brief pause, she said, "I think I was a fine girl."

Avery dug in his pocket and pulled out his roll of bills. He felt for Holly's hand, and when he put the money in her palm, she gasped.

"I got a room at the Palace Hotel," Avery said. "Room seven. Hide there and then take the next stage east. Don't ever come back, ma'am. You're still a fine girl." He reached in his other pocket and then handed her the key and said, "Let's get out of here."

Avery opened the door a crack and peered out. "You still got that knife, ma'am?" he asked.

"I think you put it on the desk."

Avery shoved the pistol in his waist band while Holly retrieved the knife.

"Wait here," he said as she handed it to him. He stepped out into the lighted hallway, his movements stiff and awkward. Turning right, he took three steps and was at the door leading into the gambling house. He took the knife, and jammed the blade between the door jam and the wall, leaving the handle blocking the door so it couldn't swing in. Holly was watching from the doorway, and when he passed her on his way back, he whispered, "Stay behind me. You know what you're gonna do?"

"Yes. I'm goin' home. Thank you … Mr. …?"

"Carson, Avery Carson of Bow City."

Avery turned and walked down the hall toward the alley. As he drew alongside the second door the click of the latch brought his heart to his throat. The door swung open, and he was face-to-face with the man Holly had called Travis. A look of shock blossomed in the man's eyes, and then he went for his gun. In one sweeping motion, Avery drew the pistol from his waist band, and before Travis's gun had cleared leather, Avery laid the heavy barrel hard against the side of his head. Travis crumpled straight down to the floor and then lurched backward into the room. Avery was stepping over him even as he fell, and he found himself looking down the barrel at two seated gunmen, both too stunned to move. A third man was slumped back in a chair, passed out with an empty bottle on the floor beside him.

"Put your hands above your head!" Avery ordered. "One wrong move and I'll bore you!"

The men did what they were told.

"Holly, drag that sack of trash in here and then close the door! You, Mr. Red Moustache," Avery snarled, "stand up slow and then turn around and put your hands on the wall. I'd just as soon kill you both, so don't tempt me!"

When the man was standing spread eagle against the wall, Avery looked at the seated man and said menacingly. "All right, mister, stand up slow, turn around, and take Red's pistol. Then throw it on the floor back here. You look back, and I'll put a hole in your head. Holly, see if there ain't a key in that fella's pocket there.

Red's pistol thumped and skidded on the floor, and Holly said, "I have the key."

"Good girl. That's my gun belt on the table. How's about you grab it and then relieve sleepin' beauty of his.

All right, Red; same thing for you. You can relieve Ugly of his pistol like he done for you. Holly, you throw their guns in the hallway, leave the key in the door." Hoping she'd play along, Avery continued. "You go fetch that scatter gun I told you about. When you got it, tap on the window there. I'll lock these rannies up and go get the horses. You wait till I come back, and if anyone shows himself at the window, cut'm in half. I'll leave the back door open, so if they try bustin' out, you got one barrel for each of 'em."

He heard Holly insert the key in the lock, and a few moments later there was a tap on the window. Avery backed up, and seeing Travis's hat on the floor, scooped it up and put it on. It sat awkwardly, and he didn't know if it was because of a poor fit or the tender welt on the back of his head. He closed and locked the door, pocketed the key, and then hurried down the hall.

Holly was at the window and, true to form, had a six gun trained on the glass. Avery noticed she was shivering as she handed him his gun belt.

"Let's go!" he said.

Once they'd made the shadows behind the hotel, he tried to give her his coat.

"I'm okay," she insisted. "I'll figure somethin' out. You got a long, cold ride ahead of you."

"No, take it, please."

Holly stubbornly shook her head, and Avery nodded grimly.

"All right," he said. "Good-bye and good luck. Come see us in Bow City sometime."

Holly stood on her tiptoes and kissed him on the cheek. Then she fled through the back door of the hotel.

CHAPTER NINETEEN

Avery buckled on his gun belt and flipped out his pistol. The weight felt right, but he stepped into the light from a back window to be sure. It was loaded. Holstering the gun, he turned and felt along the wall of the hotel, and when he came to the space between it and the next building, he turned toward the street. Pausing briefly before stepping up onto the boardwalk, he looked both ways. Crowds of people milled in front of several lighted buildings, but he stepped out boldly and cut across to the barn.

As before, the front doors were wide open, and a light was still burning. Avery drew his gun as he entered and stepped quickly to the side, dropping to one knee, but no one was in the barn. Several horses turned to eye him as he reached out and grabbed a stall rail. Pulling himself back to his feet, he holstered his pistol. At this point, speed was more important than caution, and he hurried to his horse, gritting his teeth against the pain as he threw on his saddle. His eyes darted between the front and back door as he did up his cinch, and he couldn't believe how his luck was holding.

"Maybe it ain't luck," he said under his breath. He bridled up, and as he backed his horse into the alley, he spied his crumpled hat lying on the straw. He stooped and picked it up; pushed out the crown; and then, tossing Travis's hat aside, put it gingerly on his head. He was about to mount up when he heard running footsteps on the street.

Reckless and wild, a hatless Travis pounded through the door, skidding to a stop as he raised his pistol, his face a mask of hatred. Avery crouched forward, his hand streaking down and up. His pistol bucked and blossomed flame as wood splinters stung his face. Travis's body jerked back and off line, and as he tried to bring his gun to bear, it slipped from his fingers. He took a crazy lurching step forward before falling hard to his face. Even as he hit the ground, Avery was swinging up onto his horse.

He burst through the back door into a curtain of darkness, leaving behind a melee of twisting, panic-stricken horses. Two shots stabbed the night as he struggled to find his off stirrup, and then a rail fence loomed ahead and his horse gave a mighty, hurtling leap up and over. Avery heard the back hooves clip the top rail, and then they landed with an impact that almost drove him from the saddle. He cried out involuntarily as intense pain ripped through his side and his face slammed into his horse's neck. He managed to right himself, and as another shot hammered out behind him, he took the alley east at a dead run.

At the outskirts of town, he pulled up, his horse breathing hard. He stopped to listen and then, moving at a cautious walk, turned north. Once he reached the gravely slopes where the tarpaper shacks at the edge of town petered out, he turned back west. He cocked his head as a sudden burst of shouting erupted on the main street, followed by hoof beats pounding down the road to the east, but here, all was dark and still. When he found the trail from earlier in the evening, he began the long, steady climb up and out of the valley. He felt a welcome relief when the lights of town were lost from sight behind the shoulder of the hill, and then he remembered this was only the beginning.

Glancing at the sky, he located the Big Dipper and then the North Star. With a stubborn set to his jaw, he put the buckskin into a mile-eating trot, a surprisingly warm breeze on his left cheek. Most of the snow had disappeared, and only a few scattered white patches showed against a dark backdrop. With the motion of his horse, Avery's head began to throb, and the pain in his side grew sharper and more intense. Up down, up down, up down, thump thump thump thump; his head was pounding, and his stomach grew nauseous. On and on he rode. He glanced at the Big Dipper and was disheartened to see less than an hour had passed.

Up down, up down, his stomach began to kick, and he pulled his horse to a stop, lurched from the saddle, and fell to his hands and knees, retching violently. He rolled over on his back and stared at the sky; warm saliva clinging to his cheek that he didn't bother to wipe away. The need came strong again, and he rolled over, his stomach heaving, but this time, nothing came. The convulsions tore at his side, and his head began to swim as his arms caved in beneath him. He lay there, his face in the dirt, the smell of vomit in his nostrils, and then he willed himself to his feet. He stood, swaying unsteadily and then, in a shuffling walk, went to his horse, which was contentedly cropping grass by the side of the trail. Avery realized his stomach felt better, and for this, he was thankful. With great effort and determination, he crawled back into the saddle, moving out first at a walk and then a trot.

He rode in a stupor, hardly aware of time and place. When he did remember to look at the sky, he was surprised to find that three more hours had passed. He knew he'd eventually have to stop and rest, even if only for a short while, as his horse would need time to graze. He set himself the goal of reaching his last night's campsite, though he knew it would be well past sunrise, and he stubbornly stuck to his plan.

The pain in his side settled down to a constant, numb throbbing, and then after what seemed like forever, he noticed a dull, gray light on the eastern horizon. At first it lifted his spirits, but it soon had the opposite effect, as it seemed the day was unbelievably slow in coming. The trail grew steeper, and he was forced to alternate between a walk and a trot to save his horse. A lone bird tested the reluctant morning with a tentative song, and then, all at once, birds were singing, and he broke into the small clearing near the top of the rise. The first rays of sunshine hit the slopes to the west as Avery slid from the saddle. It was all he could do to untie his bedroll, and he spread it where it fell. After loosening his cinch, he crawled between his blankets and slept.

He woke to the sound of running water and sunshine on his face. Slowly turning his head, he saw his horse standing head down and reins trailing a few feet away, and he realized then that he'd forgotten to hobble him.

"You're a good fella," Avery said. "Why you'd want to stick with a man like me I'll never know. Maybe you're Emily's angel."

The horse eyed him for a moment and then, as if realizing what was ahead, went back to grazing. Avery got stiffly to his feet and saw that the grass in the clearing had pretty much been eaten off. He fetched a can of tomatoes from his saddle bags, ate them with his fingers, and then drank the juice. He washed his hands in the creek and, using the empty can for a dipper, gulped down some cold, clean water. Glancing at the sky, he guessed he'd slept for about three hours, and he felt surprisingly refreshed. Minutes later he was back in the saddle and making good time.

Avery reached his cabin just after dark, and though he was tempted to press on, he knew a short rest would do both him and his horse good. He didn't realize just how tired and used-up he was till he stepped out of the saddle. His knees buckled under him, and he had to reach out and grab the horn to steady himself. The quick movement made him wince, and he stood there a moment to gather strength before he off saddled.

Hoping his horse would stay close but too tired to do anything about it, he turned the buckskin loose in the pasture. Once in the cabin, he stubbornly willed himself to start a fire and cook a hot meal. Later, when he was seated at the table with a plate of bacon and beans, warmed-up biscuits, and a hot cup of coffee, he was glad that he had. When he finished eating, he grabbed some blankets, and with the lamp still burning, lay down on the bearskin rug. He was afraid that, if he got into bed, he wouldn't wake up till spring.

He woke from a dead sleep to a horse whinnying. It was still dark outside, and he got slowly to his feet and then went to the door. He could see nothing, but the horse whinnied again. Judging by the stars, it was after four in the morning, and he decided he'd best get moving. He kindled the fire but then grew restless and impatient and drank the remainder of last night's coffee cold and chewed on a dry biscuit. Glancing down, he realized the front of his shirt was flecked with dried vomit, so he went quickly to the bedroom, stripped down, and put on a fresh change of clothes. As he stepped into the night, the horse whinnied a third time. Curious, Avery picked up his bridle, and headed for the pasture.

The buckskin was standing alone a few feet from the gate, looking off uphill, his ears perked forward. No doubt he was calling to the other horses, and Avery wondered at the fact that he'd not gone to them. He caught the horse and led him through the gate. As he was saddling up, he realized his head was hardly bothering him and the pain in his side was easier to ignore. *I guess the sleep did me good*, he thought.

With what lay behind him, the ride to Bow City seemed like a short one, and he moved out at an easy lope. He wondered what he'd find when he got there, and he hoped he was on time. Now that he was feeling better, it was easy to second-guess his decision to stop and sleep. A new sense of urgency rose within him, and he urged the horse into a faster run.

He made the Double Diamond in a little less than three hours, his horse lathered up but moving with a smooth, easy rhythm. About half a mile ahead in the gathering light, he spotted a buggy with two outriders, and in a matter of minutes he overtook them. It was Albert Ball and Carol, accompanied by Higgins and a rider he didn't know. Avery pulled alongside, and Ball drew his team to a stop.

He looked at Avery and new something was wrong. "What's up?" he asked.

"I think Emily's in trouble."

"How could you know?"

"It's a long story. Emily's got a past that's tryin' to catch up with her, and God help me, I ain't gonna let it."

"There's blood in your hair!" Carol exclaimed.

"I reckon there could be, ma'am."

"What can we do?" Ball asked.

"I don't rightly know what to expect. He won't be

alone though." Avery didn't mention who "he" was, and Ball didn't ask.

"Higgins, Chambers," Ball barked. "You ride on ahead with Carson. We won't be far behind."

"Thanks, Ball," Avery said.

He was just moving out when Ball said, "Carson."

Avery reined in and turned to face him.

"You're not alone here; remember that. There's plenty that will side you if need be."

Avery nodded and said, "That means a lot, Ball. It really does."

The buckskin was fidgety and anxious to be moving. Avery touched his hat brim to Carol and then moved out at a fast trot and, with his horse pushing on his hands, broke into a lope. The other two riders fell in behind.

They rode for an hour in silence, alternating between a lope and a trot, and when Avery slowed to a walk, Higgins and Chambers rode up beside him.

"Boys," he said, "in a little over a week, I'm gettin' married to as fine a lady as you could hope to meet. There's a fella comin' to Bow City wants to drag my woman back into a past she don't want no part of. I hope he hasn't come and gone."

"Young Armstead was in town yesterday," Higgins said. "He never mentioned anythin', so I reckon she's still there."

Avery nodded grimly. "That's good to know," he said. "I want to warn you boys that this fella's plenty dangerous. He's a big man where he comes from, and he's used to havin' things his way. I had a run-in with some of his boys a couple of nights back, and it was a killin' thing. I don't expect this'll be any different."

Both men watched Avery but said nothing.

"What I'm tryin' to tell you is that you might be riskin' your life by stickin' your neck in this. You're under no obligation."

"Mrs. Harper's one of ours the way I see it," Higgins said. "We look out for our own."

"I feel the same way," Chambers said. "Let's ride."

Twenty minutes later they sighted Bow City, and as they drew nearer, Avery saw two heavy wagons down the street pulled up in front of the barn. He reined in the buckskin, an iron set to his jaw and his eyes dark.

As the other two men pulled up beside him, he said quietly, "We're right on time, boys." He motioned with his chin and continued, "He's bound to have some men with them wagons. You two head on up the street and make sure they stay put. I'll head over to Emily's and see if she's there."

They moved out three abreast, traveling at a walk. As they entered the town, Avery glanced down the street toward Emily's and felt a tightness grip his chest.

"We're none too early," he said.

A wagon was pulled up in front of the Harper house, and two saddle horses stood nearby, the morning sun shining on their flanks and hips. Avery could see movement on the ground but couldn't make out what was happening.

Seeing it, Higgins said, "Chambers, you ride up the street like Carson said. Stop in at the sheriff's office and get Ernie and then see who's loafin' in the saloon and round them up too. I'm goin' with Carson."

Avery pulled the leather thong from his pistol, and Higgins did the same. Side by side, they rode down the street to the Harper house. They pulled up beside the wagon, spreading out a little. Ahead of them and to the right of the gate, two tough-looking hands were standing by their horses. From inside the house they heard voices raised in argument, and one of them was Emily's. Avery felt his blood boil, but on the outside, he was calm and still.

He grinned at the closest rider, and motioning with his head toward the house said, "Work must be tough to come by where you come from."

The rider looked at him and, shifting his feet, said, "It pays good."

Avery was silent a moment. Then he said quietly, "Travis is dead." Motioning to the house again he continued, "Over this. Does it pay that good?"

The rider didn't say anything, and Avery spoke again. "I'll make you a promise. If you interfere here, you'll be dead too, and that goes for Mr. Dirty Shirt as well."

Just then, the front door of the house slammed open, and Emily was pushed through by a big man with jet black hair. He had her arm twisted back behind her, and his other hand gripped her neck. Emily's nose was bleeding, and Avery could see the shape of a handprint outlined in red on her cheek. When she saw Avery, hope came alive in her eyes, but O'Donnell, so engrossed in what he was doing didn't see him till he was through the front gate. When he looked up, Avery turned his horse just enough so that he could see the angel wings on the gelding's hip.

O'Donnell's eyes betrayed his shock and then became wicked pools of light. "You again," he said quietly, his voice dripping with hatred. "If this ain't the luck o' the devil."

Avery squared his horse around to face O'Donnell, who threw Emily aside. She fell to her hands and knees, crawling away whimpering, and Avery had his first good look at the man.

O'Donnell was tall and broad-shouldered, and his very presence seemed to emanate raw power. He had been good-looking once, but now, his most noticeable feature was a crooked scar that ran from the bridge of a once broken nose, under his left eye, and to a cheekbone that had been caved in. It gave the eye an odd droopy appearance, and the left side of his upper lip didn't move right when he spoke. He stood square to Avery, feet apart, his right hand hanging dangerously close to his pistol. Avery hoped he could stall, for the odds weren't in his favor. Higgins had moved off to his left to gain a better shooting lane to the gunmen on the ground, and Avery had to try to ignore them. His promise to kill them if they interfered was forgotten. He knew if it came to shooting, it was going to be a bloody mess, and his one job would be to kill Mike O'Donnell.

"I might o' known," Mike said, enjoying the moment. "I've killed you so many times in my dreams, and now all

I gotta do is decide which way's best. And to think, my little whore will get to see it too."

"Watch it!" Avery said menacingly, "That's my wife you're talkin' about."

"Your wife?!" Mike laughed. "That's even better! I suppose you remember sayin' somethin' like, 'Till death do us part.' Your wife!" he said again in disbelief. "Maybe before I kill you, I'll tell you a few stories."

Avery's eyes were on Mike, but he was aware and relieved that neither of the two gunmen had drawn their pistols, and he was thankful that Emily had enough sense to stay off to the side, out of the line of fire.

Mike continued speaking, "Maybe I should tell you one o' them stories right now. Why I remember the time—"

Avery cut him off. "Shut up, O'Donnell! You can't tell me nothin' I don't already know. I'm honored that she'll have me."

"Okay, mister!" a shrill voice spoke. "Put your hands up!"

Emily gasped.

"Stay where you are, Emily!" Avery commanded.

Peter was standing in the doorway holding an ancient Walker Colt. He held it in both hands, the muzzle tracing small circles, roughly pointing at Mike O'Donnell. The hammer was cocked back, so the threat was real.

"Do what he says!" came another voice from the house next door.

Old Mrs. Parker, a widow since the Civil War, was walking toward them, a Sharps .50 caliber on her shoulder.

233

She stopped twenty feet away, the big barrel holding steady as a rock, trained on O'Donnell.

"I've been keepin' an eye on this girl just in case trash like you don't have enough sense to leave her be! Now take yer gun out'n that holster and throw it away. If'n ya make any wrong move, I'll blast ya!"

O'Donnell didn't like it. His eyes smoldered as he looked back to Avery. "This won't change a thing," he said. "I don't lose."

Avery sat his horse, his eyes on O'Donnell. "I don't know," he said. "Your boys didn't fair too well last time they was in town."

A fleeting change of expression washed across Mike's face. "I don't know what you're talkin' about," he said.

"Drop yer gun like I done told ya, an' quit yer palaverin'!" Ya got till I count three, an' then I'm lettin' this thing off. One! … Two! …"

O'Donnell's eyes flicked up the street behind Avery, and with his thumb and forefinger, he took his pistol from its holster and threw it in the dirt. Avery felt cautious relief, and though he heard horses moving in behind him, he kept his gaze locked on O'Donnell.

"All right mister. You've been in Bow City long enough." It was Sheriff Ernie Coleman. He stepped into Avery's line of sight and stopped before he'd be outflanked by O'Donnell's gun hands. "Get back up on that wagon and get out of here!" Then, deliberately turning his back on O'Donnell, he addressed a gathering crowd. "Okay everyone. I want you all to take a good look at this man!" Without turning, he pointed back at O'Donnell. "If any of you ever see him in Bow City again, spread the word, and we'll send him packing. If he won't go, shoot him!" He turned back to face Mike and said quietly, "I've heard of you, O'Donnell. When I heard you were in town, I wondered what you were after. I should've guessed you'd be up to no good. We got a fine town here, and we aim to keep it that way. Don't you ever come back."

Eyes hot with anger, Mike hesitated and then walked toward the wagon, his jaw tight and his back rigid. Avery took a chance and glanced over his shoulder. A half circle of town's people, some mounted, some on foot, hemmed them in, grim-faced and determined. Behind them, he saw Ball's buggy coming down the street. He turned back. Emily was standing just outside the gate, her arms around Peter, who still held the big pistol hanging at his side. Their eyes met and Emily smiled, her lips quivering and tears making trails down her cheeks. Avery stepped from his horse and walked quickly to her.

"Look out!"

As Avery tried to turn, a heavy force smashed into the small of his back, driving him to the ground. He hit hard on his side beneath a crushing weight, as intense pain shot through him. Iron fingers gripped his throat, and O'Donnell's twisted face was inches from his. With his right arm pinned beneath him, Avery frantically reached over Mike's shoulder with his left arm, grabbing his face in a clawlike grip, his thumb digging into O'Donnell's eye socket. O'Donnell pulled his face up and back, and as Avery felt his grip loosen, he gave a mighty heave with his body, sending O'Donnell pitching forward off balance.

Avery was able to spin onto his face, and getting his arms under him, he humped his back, driving up with his legs. O'Donnell spilled off him onto the ground, and both men found their feet at the same time. They stood that way for a moment, and time stood still.

Like a voice in the far-off distance, Avery heard Coleman shouting for him to get out of the way, and then O'Donnell charged. Avery met him head on, swinging a short right that missed. And then they were chest to chest, arms tangled, feet back and bracing. Avery could feel O'Donnell's hot breath on his neck and the stubble of his beard on his face. The pain in his side screamed, and he heard ringing in his ears, though he couldn't remember being hit. O'Donnell gave a sudden hard twist of his shoulders, breaking his right hand free. He drove an uppercut in close that glanced off Avery's cheek and then followed with a hook that landed solidly.

Avery twisted to the side and then dropped low. Driving forward, he grabbed hold of Mike's left leg and, with his shoulder in his midsection, managed to spill the man awkwardly over his back. As O'Donnell hit the ground, Avery was on him, pinning his arms beneath his knees while hammering blows with both hands.

O'Donnell jerked his arms down to his sides and heaved up with his chest. Off balance, Avery fell forward, and Mike twisted out from underneath. Avery got quickly to his feet and turned like a cat to face Mike, crouching low, feet apart and ready. Both men stood that way, breathing hard, eyes hot with battle.

Avery heard Coleman asking, "You want me to let this go, Carson?"

Avery gave a quick nod of his head. "I got it to do," he panted.

Both men began to circle, more cautious now, though Mike's damaged face was leering and confident. Avery knew that, weakened as he was, he'd need to fight smart and try to end it quickly. Aware of the need to protect his ribs, he turned his right side away from O'Donnell and with a quick, sliding step, closed the distance, lacing a straight left to the mouth.

Expecting a retaliatory blow, he ducked quickly to the side and back, but O' Donnell just took the punch and grinned. "I see you're hurt already," he said. "You're gonna hurt a whole lot more."

Almost before he was finished speaking, Avery drove another straight left to the same place.

"You can't hurt me like that," Mike said, but he looked irritated, and there was blood in his teeth. Avery hit him a third time, and O'Donnell countered with a wide right. Avery stepped inside and hooked a vicious punch down low before stepping out and to the side. O'Donnell reached for him as he turned but missed, and then off balance, he snapped out a quick left. Avery deflected it with his left forearm, hooking a solid right to the ribs followed by a straight left to the heart. O'Donnell growled and bore in, both fists swinging. Avery landed a straight right to the face, but the momentum was too great, and soon O'Donnell was driving him back.

Avery braced himself, and for a moment, they stood

toe to toe, swinging wildly. Avery took a heavy blow over his left ear, and lights burst in his brain as he felt his knees buckle. Frantically, he stepped forward as a straight left glanced off his jaw. He gripped O'Donnell's shirtfront in an effort to keep from going down, but was thrown like a rag to the ground, and then Mike pounced.

Avery managed to turn onto his back as O'Donnell landed, getting his left arm between Mike's calf and his thigh. With almost no leverage, he twisted his shoulder up, throwing the bigger man off balance just enough to take the power from his blow. Avery bucked up with his torso, while slamming his open palm up under O'Donnell's chin. With O'Donnell straightened up, Avery hooked his left leg up and over, hoping to get it under Mike's throat to pull him off. His leg came up too high and not far enough forward, and instead of finding the throat, his spur caught O'Donnell on the bridge of the nose, ripping an ugly gash down his right cheek to his ear.

O'Donnell screamed and instinctively convulsed back, twisting away from the pain, and Avery was able to throw him off. He scrambled to his feet, and before O'Donnell was set, hammered three fast blows into the man's bloodied face. O'Donnell went to his knees, and his right hand flashed down to his boot, and then he was up, holding a long, thin, wicked-looking knife. He dove forward and low, coming in for the kill, and Avery spun to the side. With the back of his left hand, he managed to slap the knife off line, and as O'Donnell's momentum carried him forward, Avery turned at the waist, and with his feet set, landed a solid right to the side of his head. The punch hit square and flush, and Avery felt the shock of it right back to his shoulder. O'Donnell fell face-first in the dirt and didn't move.

Struggling for air, Avery staggered to where the knife lay and defiantly kicked it aside. The movement threw him off balance, and he went down on one knee. As he fought back to his feet, Emily rushed into his arms, sobbing uncontrollably. He stood there, feet apart and teetering from exhaustion, holding Emily's head to his chest with bloodied hands while she gripped his torn shirt in her fists.

People were closing in around him, and he heard voices, but he couldn't sort them out. Then he was aware of Peter standing at his side, looking up at him with eyes that betrayed a little boy's need for reassurance. He let go of Emily and kneeled down, pulling the boy to him and holding him in a fatherly embrace.

"You did real good, Peter," Avery said, still breathing heavily. "That was a brave thing you done."

"I was hiding under the bed like Ma told me to do," Peter said. "That man and Ma were fighting, and I didn't know what to do. Then when he took her outside I got out and looked out the window, and I saw you. Then I heard that man call Ma that bad word, and I remembered what you told me, so I took Ma's gun from behind the door."

Avery shook his head and smiled. He put a big hand on top of Peter's head, and Emily's hand was on his shoulder.

"I'm so lucky I'm gonna get to have you for a son, Peter. We're gonna have some good times, you an' me."

"Yes, sir," Peter said. "It's gonna be fun."

"I'm awful sorry about that, Carson." It was Sheriff Coleman. He stopped in front of Avery and put his hands on his hips, shaking his head in disgust. "I never saw that coming," he said. "One moment, he was walking to his wagon, and then just like that he turns and blindsides you."

Avery winced as he got to his feet. He put an arm around Emily's shoulder and then turned as he heard O'Donnell's wagon pulling out. A horse followed meekly behind, tied to the end gate, and O'Donnell's feet protruded from the back, flopping limply from side to side with the movement of the wagon. One of O'Donnell's riders was standing stoically in front of his horse, making no move to mount up as a crowd gathered around him.

Seeing it, Coleman shook his head and said, "I'll be right back." He strode purposefully over to the man and said, "Get on your horse and get out of here!"

"I don't reckon I will," the man said.

Coleman looked at him, exasperated. "If you stay here, you'll be sleeping in the jail."

"All right." The man stood his ground and waited a moment, and then he said, "I don't work fer O'Donnell anymore, so when you see fit to let me out, I'll be lookin' for work."

A murmur passed through the crowd, and then a woman's voice said, "We're looking to hire another man, aren't we, Daddy?" It was Carol Ball. "I'm sure there's work for you at the Double Diamond."

Avery glanced at Ball, who was still seated in his buggy. He was looking down at his feet, shaking his head.

O'Donnell's rider looked at Carol, touched his hat brim, and said, "That's the first place I'll come lookin', ma'am."

CHAPTER TWENTY

The doctor left the room, and Sheriff Coleman stepped in. "You wanted to see me?" he asked, taking a seat on Peter's bed.

Avery nodded and carefully pushed himself up into a sitting position. He was in Emily's bed, his bare torso wrapped and taped, as the doctor had said he had several ribs either cracked or broken. Emily and Peter had left for the mercantile to buy him a new shirt, as his had been torn by O'Donnell's knife. His recently washed jeans were hung on a chair in front of the kitchen stove to dry.

"How are you doing?" Coleman asked.

"I'm all right. I don't reckon I need to be in bed, but Emily insisted and I didn't feel up to arguin' the point. Anyway, I guess I can't go wanderin' around, seein' how my pants are hung out to dry."

Coleman smiled and then said, "I guess I didn't do my job so good letting O'Donnell jump you like he did, but that was one sweet fight."

"The second one in two days. Maybe it's three; I can't even remember."

Coleman raised an eyebrow and waited for Avery to continue. Avery then went on to tell him about riding south in hopes of finding some information about the man he'd buried. Briefly and concisely, he told of everything that had happened and of his race against time to get back to Bow City.

When he'd finished Coleman was leaning forward, his elbows on his knees. "So you mean to tell me the outlaw that got away was working for O'Donnell?"

"I thought you should know," Avery said.

Coleman nodded. "Marshall Claiborne in Denver is a friend of mine. He's a stubborn bulldog of a man that won't quit. I'll let him know."

Avery nodded, and Coleman got up to leave.

"So you had those broken ribs before the fight," he said. "Staples said he's glad you never took up his offer at the dance. What was that all about?"

"Nothin'," Avery said. "That boy needs to learn to take it easy on the liquor is all."

Coleman nodded. "I guess I'll go and let you get some rest," he said. "The preacher and his wife got here a week early, so I think I'll drop by and say hello."

Avery looked up with interest. "A week early you say?"

"That's right," Coleman said. "I've got O'Donnell's man in jail too, so I'd better remember to feed him."

Avery nodded, and Coleman left.

∽   ∽

Avery woke from a deep sleep and saw by the light in the window that it was late afternoon. He could hear Emily singing as she moved about her kitchen, and he felt drowsy and content. Somewhere along the line, he slipped off to sleep again, and when he opened his eyes, Emily was in the room putting clean sheets on Peter's bed. She had her back to him, and Avery found himself admiring her shape and her movements in a way he wasn't sure he should until after they were married. He forced himself to look away, and then he heard something clatter to the floor, and Emily's exasperated whisper.

Oh darn!" She turned quickly to see if she'd awakened him, and when their eyes met, her face broke into a smile. "Sorry I woke you," she said. She came to him and, leaning over, placed a soft kiss on his forehead.

When she took a seat on Peter's bed, Avery said, "You are so beautiful."

Emily smiled in a way that made him glad he'd said it. "You're not," she said, her face becoming serious. "Half your face is purple. How are you feeling? Are you comfortable?"

Avery looked at her a moment, wondering how much he should say, and then just went ahead, speaking honestly. "Actually, ma'am, I'm terrible uncomfortable."

A look of concern crossed Emily's brow, and she said, "Oh I'm sorry, Avery. Is there anything I can do?"

"No, I don't reckon there is. Not till we're married anyway."

Emily looked at him questioningly.

And then he continued. "It maybe ain't proper for me to say it, but I can't hardly look at you without wishin' you was in this bed with me."

Emily's cheeks colored a little, but then she reached over and took his hand in hers, raised it to her lips, and kissed it. "Avery," she said softly. "I love you so much. I was so afraid for you." She kissed his hand a second time and then said, "I can't wait to be married either."

Avery looked at her hopefully and said, "Coleman told me the preacher's already in town. He came a week early. How would you feel about movin' up the weddin' a bit?"

Emily smiled. "How soon?" she asked.

"How about this evenin'?"

Emily gasped and then, laughing, she said, "Avery Carson! You can't be serious!"

"Yes, ma'am, I'm awful serious. You could wear your pretty green dress for a weddin' dress, and I could stop by the mercantile and find somethin' to suit the occasion." Avery raised up on one elbow, and as the idea gained momentum, he continued enthusiastically. "Word travels fast, and I'm sure folks would show up at the church on short notice. If the preacher's willin', I think it'd be a fine idea!"

Emily looked at him and shook her head in disbelief, but her eyes were shining. "I don't even know how I want to fix my hair," she said.

"Why not make it curly like you done the night of the

dance? That was real pretty. Fact is, though, I ain't ever seen it not look pretty."

"I wouldn't have time for that anyway," Emily said, "but I guess it doesn't really matter." She thought for a moment and then, with eyes full of mischief, said, "Why not? I'll go see what Pastor Cambridge says." She got to her feet, stood, and regarded Avery for a moment, her expression thoughtful and gentle. She reached out and touched his beard-stubbled cheek with her fingers, and as her hand fell away, she said, "I shouldn't be long."

⚬⚬   ⚬⚬

It seemed that Emily was gone forever. Outside, the light was fading, and Avery grew restless and impatient. He wondered where Emily had put his new shirt, and he considered wrapping himself in a blanket to go see if his pants were dry. He was about to get out of bed when he heard the front door open, but it was a male voice he heard as footsteps approached the room.

Then Wally and Peter stepped in. "Howdy, you rabble-rouser," Wally said. "Bow City was nice and dull before you showed up."

"Have you seen Emily?" Avery asked.

"Yeah we seen her, didn't we, Peter? But you ain't gonna see her again till she's walkin' up the aisle."

"Really!" Avery exclaimed, his face lighting up as he sat up quickly. He winced momentarily, but then the pain was forgotten. "How soon is the weddin'?"

"Not for a couple hours. You can take it easy."

Avery laughed. "I can't take it easy," he said. "I need to shave and get cleaned up and then head over to the Mercantile to get some respectable clothes."

"We already got you some," Peter said enthusiastically. "I got some new clothes too!"

Avery grinned at Peter, and the grin he got in return reminded him that this was equally big for the boy.

"We picked you up a broadcloth suit," Wally said. "There wasn't much selection, so I hope it fits."

"It'll be fine I'm sure, and thanks."

They heard a light knocking on the front door, and Peter ran from the room.

Soon Carol Ball entered. "I've come to get Emily's dress," she said, her face flushed with excitement. Smiling at Avery, she shook her head in mock disgust and said, "You don't give a girl much time do you, you impulsive man!" She took the dress down from back wall, gave a little wave, and left in a hurry.

"Emily's gettin' ready over at the hotel," Wally explained. "Carol and Miriam are gonna stand up for her, and me and Peter will be standin' up for you if that's okay."

Avery looked gratefully at Wally and said, "It couldn't be better. You boys have been busy."

Wally nodded and said, "Emily got us all whipped into shape. The way she's actin', you'd think she caught herself a prize."

Avery's face became serious. "God help me, I'll do my best to make sure it's true."

Peter came into the bedroom, proudly wearing a new

pair of trousers and a white shirt that still showed the creases from having been long folded.

"Well ain't you a handsome fella!" Avery exclaimed. "I best get busy myself, or I'll be late for my own weddin'!"

As he swung his feet to the floor, Wally said, "You might have a little extra time. Ball sent Chambers out to the ranch on a fast horse to fetch in his other women folk. He said, if they missed the weddin', there'd likely be a lynchin' to follow, and it'd be his. Emily promised she'd wait."

A subdued murmur accompanied the crowded room as Avery, Peter, and Wally waited with the preacher at the front of the dimly lit church. One lantern hung from an overhead beam, and the only other light came from the candles on the altar and candles on each of the four window sills.

The sound of voices grew slightly as everyone turned their heads, and then expectant silence held the room as Carol Ball appeared in the rear entryway. She walked slowly up the aisle, enjoying the moment, and was followed a short time later by Miriam. When both women were standing at the front of the church, opposite the men, everyone in the pews stood and turned to face the entryway.

Avery swallowed and felt his pulse racing, and then an excited murmur rose again as Emily stepped through the door into the light of the room. As she walked slowly toward him, moist eyes shining and her pale hair a halo in the candlelight, Avery was overcome by a feeling that nothing on this earth could ever be more right and that he had been undeservedly blessed.

Emily's hair was pinned in loose swirls on top of her head, and she wore a string of white pearls around her bare throat. Avery returned her smile and, completely taken by her clean beauty, drew in a deep breath and breathed a prayer of thanks.

Facing her, he took her hands in his, and then her lips moved ever so slightly. "I love you," was what she said, and he couldn't stop the tears.

Before God and the people of Bow City, they made their vows to have and to hold, to honor and cherish, through all that was to come, as long as they both shall live.

EPILOGUE

veryone in Bow City said it was the mildest, most open winter in memory. It wasn't until mid-April that the snow came—wet, heavy snow that came and went over and over again, while on the mountain slopes it piled in thick and deep.

Avery and Peter left the cattle on a small knoll south of the river and rode for home. Peter was wearing a felt hat shaped like his father's and a small pair of batwing chaps that had been an early birthday present. They dismounted in front of the house with the sound of piano music coming through the walls, and Avery thought for the thousandth time that the piano had been as much a gift for him as it had been for Emily.

Emily got up from the piano as they entered, kissed them both, and said, "Lunch is in the warming oven."

"That's good, 'cause Peter here's just about faintin'." As he hung up his coat, Avery continued speaking. "I'd like to head out right away. I got a feelin' we're in for a good rain."

"Do you think the dance could get rained out?" Emily asked.

"I doubt it. Albert's likely got the loft empty by now, so they could always move inside. If you don't mind ridin', I think we'd best leave the wagon in case that rain decides to turn into another dump of snow."

"No, I don't mind riding; in fact, I'd like to. I'm all packed so we can leave right away." She put her arms around Avery's neck and he drew her to himself, kissing her while Peter waited at the table.

Emily moved her lips from his mouth to his ear and whispered, "I think I'm pregnant!"

"What!" Avery exclaimed.

"What?" Peter asked.

"Oh nothing," Emily said, still embracing Avery and smiling up at him.

"What do you mean nothing?"

"I think we better take the wagon," Avery said. "I don't know if you should be ridin'."

"I'm sure I'll be fine."

"Why can't Ma ride?"

"We'll take the wagon just to be on the safe side. Are you sure?"

Emily smiled. "Pretty sure," she said.

It was late afternoon, and the sky was dull and heavy. Three tough-looking riders rode in from the south and pulled up a few hundred yards from the buildings.

"That's got to be the place, Mike." The speaker was a tall, unkempt man with long, tangled, black hair. "What do you reckon we should do?"

Mike O'Donnell thought a moment then said, "They won't know you, Austin. Billy and I will wait out o' sight while you go have a look. I got a feelin' there's no one home. It's awful quiet, and there's no smoke from the chimney."

"I just wish I knew what them Injun's was up to," the third man said. They all turned in their saddles to look at five mounted Indians who were watching them from about half a mile away.

"Well they've done nothin' so far, so forget 'em," O'Donnell said gruffly.

"Nothin' but follow us for two days. I don't like it, Mike. I don't like it at all. That girl and the pistol fighter are bad luck, and them Injuns is part of it. I got me a feelin'."

Mike was silent. Then he turned his scarred face toward Billy and said, "Well I got a feelin' too, and it runs pretty deep. My luck's took a turn for the worse ever since that fella ran off with my woman, and it ain't gonna turn around till I do somethin' about it. That's just how it is." Turning to face the other man, he said, "Austin, go see if anyone's home. We'll wait here."

Austin nodded, and as O'Donnell watched him ride away, the third man spoke again. "I'll say this, and then that'll be the end of it. You're the boss, and you've always done right by me."

"Okay, I'm listenin'," Mike said, as he turned to watch the Indians.

"I didn't bust you out of jail just so my hair would be hangin' from some tepee pole. If there's five Injuns, there's bound to be more. I reckon they're just waitin' for some of their friends to join 'em, and then they plan on killin' us. It ain't natural the way they're actin'. Somethin' ain't right here, just like it's never right where that woman's concerned. I say we forget her and head for the gold fields of Montana."

O'Donnell's horse shook its head and snorted. Austin was on his way back, moving at a trot.

"You could be right, Billy. Just the same, I ain't movin' on till I've killed 'em both. That's when my luck will turn. You'll see."

"No one's home," Austin said as he pulled up. He glanced nervously at the Indians and then continued speaking. "A wagon with one outrider headed out a few hours ago though."

"Okay, we'll follow 'em," O'Donnell said. "They'll be back, and we'll find a good spot for an ambush. We'll soon need to make camp anyway."

"Why not wait for 'em in the house?"

Mike glanced at the house and then at the sky. "It's temptin'," he said. Then turning to watch the Indians he continued. "I just wonder if that ain't what they're waitin' for though. Once we're inside, they could run off our horses, and then we'd be pinned down. I think we'd best keep movin'."

About half a mile past the buildings, Austin turned

in the saddle and said, "Hey, them Injuns ain't followin' us no more."

A smile creased O'Donnell's crooked face, and he said, "See Billy, our luck's turnin' already."

A short time later, they rode into the gap, and a light drizzle began to fall.

"Look there, down by the river," O'Donnell said, pointing. "There's a big rock overhang, so we'll be able to stay out o' the rain and keep a fire going. The pass is narrow here, so they'll have to come right past us. It's perfect."

Billy cast a wary eye at the overcast sky but said nothing. He'd said enough already, and Mike knew what he was doing.

∽ ∽

At the Double Diamond, the rain turned to a downpour and drove everyone inside. As Avery had predicted, the dancers took to the barn loft, and it was hard to hear the fiddle music over the sound of the rain on the roof. He was just guiding Emily from the dance floor when Albert Ball approached.

"The wife's got a bed for you two up at the house," he said. "I reckon you might need it for a couple or three nights anyway."

"Why's that?" Emily asked.

"This rain's gonna melt that snowpack in a hurry. There'll be a flood like we've never seen in this country. You may not get through that pass for a week."

"I think you're right," Avery said, "and thanks for the bed, but we can head for town in the mornin'. I hate to put you out."

"Nonsense. It'll be nice to have a visit. If this rain keeps up, we won't be workin' for a few days anyway."

Avery nodded. "How's your new man been workin' out?" he asked.

"Real good. He's a good hand."

"He's a good dancer too I see," Emily said.

They all turned to look at the dance floor, where Carol was dancing with the man who'd ridden into Bow City with O'Donnell last fall.

Ball smiled and shrugged his shoulders. "What can I say? I think he's a good man too."

∾ ∾

The following morning, the rain was still coming down. Ball came in for the noon meal and told everyone that a horse with a saddle under its belly had wandered in during the night. One of his hands had backtracked it and lost the trail up close to the pass. He'd told him that the river was, "roarin' like the wrath of God, poundin' and boilin' through the pass a good thirty feet above the trail. It was a scary thing to behold."

CPSIA information can be obtained
at www.ICGtesting.com
Printed in the USA
LVOW10s0829041216
515001LV00004B/1/P